"Shh! Someone's coming," Joe whispered to Samantha and Wishbone.

Joe slunk down farther in the bushes. Next to him, he could feel Sam trying to scrunch down in the darkness. Out of the corner of his eye, he saw Wishbone flattening himself to the ground.

The footsteps continued to come closer, but Joe couldn't see who was there. It was getting harder to see by the minute, and the bushes were blocking his vision.

Looking up, Joe could see that it was a man, but he couldn't make out the face. The guy headed for the back door of the warehouse and disappeared inside. Sam pulled out her camera. The three of them huddled together and waited.

A few minutes later, the guy came back out again carrying a large box. He walked away from the warehouse.

"He's getting away!" Joe whispered to Sam.

Sam stood up, pointed her camera straight at the guy, and snapped. . . .

Other books in the
wishbone™ Mysteries series:

*coming soon

WISHBONE Mysteries

LIGHTS! CAMERA! ACTION DOG!

by Nancy Butcher

WISHBONE™ created by Rick Duffield

Big Red Chair Books™, *A Division of **Lyrick Publishing**™*

This book is a work of fiction. The characters, incidents, and dialogues are products of the author's imagination and are not to be construed as real. Any resemblance to actual events or persons, living or dead, is entirely coincidental.

 Big Red Chair Books™, *A Division of Lyrick Publishing*™
300 E. Bethany Drive, Allen, Texas 75002

©1998 Big Feats! Entertainment

Edited by Kevin Ryan

Copy edited by Jonathon Brodman

Cover concept and design by Lyle Miller

Interior illustrations by Kathryn Yingling

Wishbone photograph by Carol Kaelson

Library of Congress Catalog Card Number: 98-84944

ISBN: 1-57064-289-3

First printing: August 1998

10 9 8 7 6 5 4 3 2 1

Printed in the United States of America

*For Philip
and Christopher*

FROM THE BIG RED CHAIR . . .

Oh . . . hi! Wishbone here. You caught me right in the middle of some of my favorite things—books. Let me welcome you to the WISHBONE MYSTERIES. In each story, I help my human friends solve a puzzling mystery. In *LIGHTS! CAMERA! ACTION DOG!*, Joe gets a small part in a movie that is being made in Oakdale. The filming is delayed because of vandalism on the set. Joe and Wishbone race to discover the truth before the producers decide to shut down production!

The story takes place late in the summer, just before the events that you'll see in the second season of my WISHBONE television show. In this story, Joe is fourteen, and he and his friends will be entering the eighth grade. Like me, they are always ready for adventure . . . and a good mystery.

You're in for a real treat, so pull up a chair and a snack and sink your teeth into *LIGHTS! CAMERA! ACTION DOG!*

Chapter One

Wishbone ran down the street, his paws in over-drive and his fur flying in the wind. It was a beautiful summer Sunday afternoon, the kind that made him feel especially glad to be a dog. The sky was bright blue, and the air was full of delicious smells. Up ahead, a lawn sprinkler was practically begging for him to run through the water it sprayed.

"Coming through!" Wishbone announced, speeding up. A spray of cool water rained down along his fur. Wishbone barked with excitement. "I'd stick around and do this some more, but I've got someplace I've gotta be!" he added.

"Wishbone! Wait up!"

Wishbone turned around. His tail went into a high-speed wag. His best friend in the world and room-mate, Joe Talbot, was cycling up the street toward him. Samantha Kepler, one of Joe's human best friends, was close behind on her bike. Wishbone liked Sam. She was always ready to help a person or dog in need, she had a great sense of adventure, and she wasn't stingy at all with snacks.

"What's your hurry, Wishbone?" Joe called out breathlessly. He braked to a stop next to the little white-with-brown-and-black-spots Jack Russell terrier. Joe leaned down to scratch his pal's ears. The boy had a tall, athletic build, a lean, handsome face, and big brown eyes. He was dressed in khaki pants and a faded blue shirt that said OAKDALE SPORTS & GAMES. A shiny black bike safety helmet covered his brown hair.

"That's good. . . . No, more to the left. *There!*" Wishbone sighed happily as Joe continued to scratch. "I *was* in a hurry, Joe, but I'm always happy to take a little break."

"I'm sure Wishbone's as eager as we are to get there," Sam said, stopping her bike next to Joe's. Sam had silky blond hair pulled back in a ponytail, and friendly hazel eyes. She wore a red T-shirt, cutoffs, and a white bike safety helmet.

"I guess so," Joe said, smiling. "He's never seen a movie set."

Simon Moore was all Oakdale had been talking about for weeks—or it seemed that way to Wishbone, anyway. Two brothers—Connor and Billy Drake, both Oakdale natives and recent film-school graduates— had come home to make a movie about a man named Simon Moore. He had been mayor of Oakdale in the 1880s. A warehouse near downtown Oakdale had been made into a Victorian-era movie set. Several local residents had been given minor roles in the film. Today was the first day of the shoot.

Wishbone had heard Joe's mom, Ellen, mention

that the real-life Simon Moore had been only eighteen years old when he became mayor. *That's only four years older than Joe and Sam!* Wishbone thought.

"I hope I get lots of good photos of the cast and crew," Sam said, patting her backpack. Wishbone could see the strap of her 35-millimeter camera poking out of it. "They'll be great for the first issue of the school paper in the fall."

Wishbone, Joe, and Sam headed for downtown Oakdale, with Wishbone in the lead. The little dog raced ahead. First, the Oakdale post office came into view, then Main Street, then his favorite restaurant in the whole world, Pepper Pete's Pizza Parlor. Sam's dad, Walter, owned Pepper Pete's, and Sam worked there part-time. Wishbone thought that the pizza parlor's liberal "dogs welcome" policy was great. He also approved of Sam's personal policy of slipping him leftovers.

Wishbone raised his nose in the air and inhaled deeply. "Ah, pepperoni and sausage and cheese—some of my favorite smells," he said. "Hey, guys—what do you say we stop at Pepper Pete's for lunch before we head over to the set? I know we already *had* lunch, but you can never have too much of a good thing, right?"

Just then, Wishbone's attention shifted because of something new and strange. He glanced around quickly, sniffing strongly. Main Street was jammed with the usual weekend crowd: dogs checking out trees, adults shopping, kids cycling and skateboarding. But there was something new in the air . . . something Wishbone wasn't used to smelling in the heart of downtown Oakdale.

It was the combined scents of hay, sweat, and manure.

"Horses!" Wishbone concluded. "Huh? But why would there be horses in downtown Oakdale?"

Joe and Sam braked to a stop. "Look, Joe!" Sam exclaimed. She pointed down the street, where a pair of horses suddenly came into view. They were pulling a big brown carriage.

Wishbone, Joe, and Sam didn't move from where they were. They watched the carriage slowly make its way down Main Street. Cars stopped, grown-ups stared, and children cheered. As the carriage neared, the smells of hay, sweat, and manure grew stronger. The steady, rhythmic clip-clop sound of hooves became louder.

The driver of the carriage was dressed in a faded brown suit. He had pulled a scruffy brown cap low over his forehead. Wishbone could just make out a big, drooping black moustache beneath the driver's nose.

"That guy looks familiar," Wishbone said, sitting down on his haunches. "I know! Hey, Joe! That's the guy who works at Jack's Service Station!"

Joe elbowed Sam. "Hey, that's the guy who works at Jack's Service Station!"

"I just *said* that," Wishbone pointed out. "No one ever listens to the dog," he added with a sigh.

"A horse-drawn carriage—it's like something out of a movie," Sam said with a smile. Then her eyes lit up. "Wait a second—this really *is* out of a movie. I bet the carriage is being used in the film *Simon Moore!* The guy from Jack's must be one of the people who got a bit part in the movie."

Just then, Wishbone heard a woman's voice call out to them. "Joe! Sam! Isn't this the most exciting thing in the whole world?"

Wishbone could recognize that voice anywhere—as well as the familiar scent of petunias and potting soil. They belonged to Wanda Gilmore, Wishbone and Joe's next-door neighbor. Wanda had a great garden for burying bones and chew toys. However, for some strange reason, *she* chose to plant flowers there.

Wishbone looked up at Wanda, who was walking quickly up the sidewalk toward them, waving. She wore a straw hat covered with plastic fruit, and had on a bright pink sundress. There was a big black camera hanging from a strap around her neck.

"Hi, Miss Gilmore," Joe and Sam said at the same time.

"Isn't this *fabulous,* kids?" Wanda cried out. "A movie about old Oakdale being filmed right here in our own town!" Wanda was the president of the Oakdale Historical Society, and she loved anything that had to do with local history.

"We're on our way to the set right now," Sam told her. "I'm going to take some pictures for the first fall edition of the school paper."

Wanda patted her camera. "Great idea, Sam. I'm going to get over there later today and get some shots for tomorrow's edition of the *Chronicle.*" Besides loving Oakdale history, Wanda was also the publisher of the local paper. Wishbone kept meaning to talk to her about starting a new column that would cover dog news only. *One of these days,* he thought.

The carriage passed the group at that moment.

Wishbone jumped back as eight horse hooves, then four big, rickety-looking wheels, rumbled past. A single passenger, a woman, looked out of a window and gave a little wave. She was wearing white-lace gloves and a hat with a feather in it. Her old-fashioned purple dress had a high, buttoned collar.

Wanda and Sam began to snap pictures with great enthusiasm. The crowd watching the scene clapped and whistled. "That was cool," Joe said, staring after the carriage as it drove away.

"Definitely," Sam agreed. She tucked her camera back inside her backpack. "Now I'm *really* psyched about seeing the set. Come on!"

"'Bye, kids," Wanda said. She pulled a note pad and pen out of her purse. "I'm going to interview the crowd and see what they think of all this. Make sure to look for the story in tomorrow's *Chronicle!*" She turned to a young couple and began asking them a whole list of questions.

"Let's go, Wishbone," Joe said, starting down the street on his bike.

"I'm way ahead of you, Joe," Wishbone said, trotting into the lead.

A few minutes later, Wishbone and his friends found themselves outside the large warehouse that had been rented for the *Simon Moore* movie. Near the doorway, a man wearing an old-fashioned-looking gray suit and a matching round derby hat was pacing back and forth, with a film script in hand.

"Mayor, we *must* dig deeper into our pockets if we want to save Oakdale," the man recited, shaking his fist. "Mayor, we must *dig deeper* into our pockets if we want to save Oakdale," he repeated with more emphasis, shaking his fist again.

"Did you mention digging? Where do I sign up?" Wishbone said, his tail wagging wildly.

The man glanced up at Joe and Sam, who were locking up their bikes. "Oh, hello," he said in a tired voice.

"Hi," Sam said, moving away from her bike. "I'm here to take some pictures of the cast and crew for our school paper. I talked to the director on the phone yesterday, and he said it would be okay."

"We're taking a break from shooting, so you could probably go right on in," the man said. "But I must warn you—Connor's not in a good mood. We're shooting this scene for the twelfth time. Can you imagine! Twelve takes, and we still don't have the scene nailed down. Nothing seems to be going right today." Then he continued pacing and shaking his fist. "Mayor, *we* must dig deeper," he went on, reciting his line in yet another way, with different emphasis.

Joe and Sam exchanged a glance and smiled. Then Joe swung open the heavy metal door and entered the warehouse. Sam and Wishbone followed. Sam fingered her camera nervously. Wishbone sniffed the air with eager anticipation.

"Oh, boy!" Wishbone exclaimed once they were inside. His tail began to wag a mile a minute. "Check this out, guys!"

Wishbone had been in this very warehouse

recently, when Joe had biked through the area on his way to a friend's house. The door had been open, and Wishbone had poked his head inside to do some investigative sniffing. The place had contained nothing but piles and piles of dusty boxes.

But since then, it had been completely changed. Now, there were bright movie lights shining overhead, thick electrical cables snaking everywhere, and lots of complicated-looking film-making equipment. There were actors in 1880s Victorian-era costumes rehearsing their lines. Crew members with notes and papers attached to their clipboards ran around excitedly.

It reminded Wishbone of the time he had been in a TV dog food commercial as Mr. MacPooch—well, he had *almost* been in the commercial. That experience had been a disaster. Wishbone had decided then that show business was not for him.

You'll never catch me in front of a camera again, Wishbone thought, glancing suspiciously at one of the

big black movie cameras. Still, he couldn't help but feel curious and excited about the busy scene before him.

In the center of the warehouse was the actual film set: a beautiful Victorian living room—called a drawing room back then, Wishbone remembered. Two men dressed in old-fashioned-looking suits were sitting on a red-velvet couch. They were drinking what looked like iced tea out of disposable plastic cups. A woman in jeans and a T-shirt was racing back and forth between them, powdering their noses with a brush.

A young blond-haired man wearing khaki slacks and a pressed white shirt was standing over the two actors, his arms crossed over his chest. "You have this scene all wrong," he said to them. "*All* wrong. You're not acting out a tea party. You're acting out a very tense meeting between two opponents who are about to become unwilling partners in crime. Got it?"

The guy seemed like a bully to Wishbone. *Kind of like Bruno the Doberman when he's around other dogs,* he thought.

Just then, another young man hurried by, nearly stepping on Wishbone's front paws as he went. "I already had my nails clipped this month, thank you," Wishbone said, jumping back.

"Connor, I can't get hold of a smoke-making machine until Wednesday," the guy said to the blond-haired man. Wishbone noticed that the two of them looked a lot alike. But the one in a hurry was dressed very casually in a baseball shirt, baseball cap, and cut-off jeans. "I told my guy we'd throw in a free *Simon Moore* T-shirt if he could get it for us by tomorrow, but he didn't bite," the guy added with a grin.

16

"We *have* to have the smoke machine tomorrow, Billy. Get him back on the phone!" Connor snapped.

"All right, all right," Billy replied good-naturedly. "Maybe he'll go for *two* free T-shirts and a baseball cap."

Just then, one of the actors on the red-velvet couch dropped his cup, and liquid and ice cubes splattered everywhere. "Oh, great!" he muttered.

Billy raised a walkie-talkie to his lips and pressed a button. "Please get a mop in here—pronto!" Then he turned to the actor. "I know the drinks are bad here, but they're not *that* bad," he joked.

Wishbone cocked his head. "If that was chicken soup, I'd help you guys clean up, but I don't do iced drinks."

"Connor, I refuse to wear this ridiculous, uncomfortable wig!" an actress complained from the sidelines. She tugged at the mass of heavy blond curls sitting on her head.

"And I want to talk to you about changing some of my lines," another actress piped up.

"Wow! It's nuts in here," Joe whispered to Sam, as a phone began to ring shrilly.

"I think what everyone needs is a nice, long, soothing snack break," Wishbone remarked. "It always works for me!"

Sam pointed toward Connor, who was trying to hold several conversations at once. "That must be Connor Drake, the director and producer of *Simon Moore*," she whispered to Joe. "He's the one I talked to yesterday. The one with the walkie-talkie must be his brother, Billy. He wrote the script, and he's also the A.D."

Joe frowned. "What's an A.D.?"

"Assistant director," Sam replied. "Connor explained the position to me. The A.D. helps the director keep things running smoothly on the set."

"Come on, people, let's take this scene from the top," Connor said suddenly, glancing at his watch. Then he fixed his eyes on Wishbone and his friends. "Uh . . . excuse me, but who are you?"

"I'm Wishbone, and I'm here to inspect your craft-services table," Wishbone explained. He turned to Joe and Sam. "In case you don't know, *craft services* is show-business language for 'the sacred place where the snacks are kept.'"

"I'm Samantha Kepler, and this is Joe Talbot. I talked to you about taking some pictures of the cast and crew," Sam told Connor.

"Oh, right, right. Listen, please have a seat and just wait. It's going to be a minute." Connor turned back to his actors and was about to say something when Billy interrupted him again.

"Uh . . . that was Paul Mathers on the line," Billy announced, holding up a cell phone. "He's not going to be able to make it for tomorrow's scene—or any other scene, for that matter." He stared at his brother, waiting for some reaction.

"What are you talking about? Why not?" Connor kept his voice low, but Wishbone could hear the anger and tension bubbling up in it.

"Seems he got a better job offer," Billy replied, shrugging. "But that's show business, right? Or that's low-budget show business, anyway."

Connor's jaw dropped. "You mean he decided to work on another movie?"

"It's a small part in Roz Romero's new movie," Billy explained. "A *well-paying* part. Paul's cousin's girlfriend knows the casting director . . . or maybe it was Paul's girlfriend's cousin—I forget."

"Wow! Roz Romero," Sam whispered to Joe. "She's a famous movie director."

"I don't care if he got the *lead* in that film," Connor snapped at his brother. "He made a commitment to be in *our* movie." He stabbed a finger in the direction of Billy's cell phone. "Get him on the line for me, Billy. Let me talk to him."

"Uh . . . you kind of can't," Billy said slowly. "He was calling from the airport. He's on his way to North Carolina for the shoot."

Uh-oh, Connor looks as if he's about to explode, Wishbone thought, glancing at the director. His face was beet-red, and he looked furious.

"Well, *who's* going to play Beau Smith's son, then?" Connor demanded.

"We'll just have to recast the role." Billy put his hand on Connor's arm. "Come on, Con, we can deal with this. It's not the end of the world."

"What do you mean, it's not the end of the world?" Connor was practically shouting now. All the cast and crew members were staring at him. "We're behind schedule as it is, and it's only the first day of filming!" he said angrily. "This production is canceled! I've had it!" With that, he turned on his heels and stormed off the set.

19

Chapter Two

Joe watched Billy glance uneasily at the twenty or so cast and crew members. All of them were staring at Connor in shock. Then Billy raced after Connor and caught him by the elbow. "We need to talk," he whispered. To the others, he called out, "Uh . . . everybody run through your lines one more time!"

"It'll take more than another run-through to get *this* film on track," one of the actors muttered under his breath.

Joe watched as Connor and Billy moved into a corner and began to talk in hushed voices. Although Joe had watched lots of movies in his life, he'd never actually seen one being made before. He had no idea that the process could be so difficult and so tense.

He also wondered about Connor, who seemed very tough and short-tempered. *He must not be very easy to work with,* Joe thought. *He doesn't even seem to be nice to his own brother. But Billy seems to take his brother's temper good-naturedly.*

Then Joe noticed that Wishbone was belly-crawling to where the Drake brothers were having their private conversation. "What are you doing, boy?" Joe whispered, moving toward him.

As Joe got closer to Wishbone, he began to catch bits and pieces of Connor and Billy's discussion: phrases like "schedule delays" and "last scene" and "money problems."

"I didn't mean to lose my temper like that, Billy," Connor was saying. "But today has been a total disaster. Half the actors don't know their lines, and the other half don't *like* theirs. Our cameraman is upset because he wants to do this scene with a hand-held camera. What's-his-name—who handles all the props—gets food poisoning. We can't seem to track down a smoke machine. And now Paul Mathers

decides to drop out." Connor sighed and shook his head. "Maybe the man we spoke to earlier on the phone was right, Billy."

"Shh! We can't let word get out about that phone call," Billy said quickly. "What if Mrs. Crabbe finds out? That could mean the end of . . ."

Billy lowered his voice at this point. Joe couldn't hear the rest of their conversation. *What phone call?* he wondered. *The end of what? And who's Mrs. Crabbe?*

Joe glanced over at Sam, who was using the break to snap some pictures of the set. Sam was a great photographer, and she always looked happy when she had a camera in hand.

Joe started to walk toward her, to tell her about Connor and Billy's puzzling conversation. Suddenly, he felt a tap on his shoulder.

"Excuse me."

Joe turned around. Billy was standing there. Joe gulped, wondering if he was going to get into trouble for eavesdropping.

"I . . . uh—" Joe began.

Billy cocked his head and stared at Joe. "I'm Billy Drake," he said. "Assistant director, scriptwriter, and all-around talented guy. I've got a question for you: Have you ever done any acting?"

Joe was taken completely by surprise. "Acting? Uh . . . no, not really. I was in a school play in fourth grade, but that's about it."

"A school play . . . that's cool," Billy said, stuffing his hands into his pockets and smiling. "What was it about?"

"Uh . . . it was this play written by students. It

was about a kid who thinks there's a dinosaur living in his backyard."

Joe had no idea where this line of questioning was going. *Why does Billy want to stand around talking about my school play when he and Connor are having a crisis?* he wondered.

"I bet you were the star, weren't you?" Billy asked Joe. "I can just picture you now: 'But Mom, Dad, I'm telling you,'" he cried out, imitating Joe's voice almost exactly, "'I really *did* see a *T rex* behind the tool shed!'"

Joe laughed. "Actually, I played the dinosaur. It wasn't much of a part. I had to wear this costume that made me really hot and sweaty. Oh, yeah, and the tail fell off during the performance."

Billy slapped Joe on the shoulder. "See? That just goes to show you that there are problems with *every* production," he said with a smile. Then he waved to Connor, who had gone over to talk to a couple of actors. "Connor! I've got a new Byron Smith for you! What's your name?" he added, turning back to Joe.

"Uh . . . Joe Talbot," Joe said. *Byron Smith? What's Billy talking about?* he wondered.

Connor came over, his arms crossed over his chest. Seeing him side by side with Billy, Joe was struck by the close physical resemblance between them. They both had the same tall, slender build, dark blond hair, and intense blue-gray eyes. Connor seemed to be the buttoned-down-shirt-and-khaki-pants kind of guy, whereas Billy seemed to be more comfortable in his worn-looking baseball shirt and cap.

Connor is definitely the serious one, Joe thought.

Billy's the opposite. He seems pretty easygoing. And he's funny, with a nice sense of humor.

Connor glanced at Joe, then at Billy. "Byron Smith? You mean . . . *him?*" He pointed to Joe.

"This is Joe Talbot," Billy explained patiently. "He has some acting experience"—Joe was about to protest, but Billy didn't give him a chance—"and you have to admit, he's perfect for the role," Billy went on. "The right age, the right look."

Connor fixed his eyes on Joe. "Joe and I were introduced earlier. Do you have your acting résumé and head-shot photos with you?"

"I . . . uh—" Joe stammered.

"It's a simple part, Connor," Billy interrupted. "A few lines here and there. He'll be fine."

Connor frowned. "I don't know. . . . I was thinking that we should call John DeMarco. He might be willing to fill in."

"Connor, do you really think that's a practical idea? John's in New York. It could take him days to make arrangements to get here—*if* he's even available. And we don't exactly have enough money to fly him in and make a hotel reservation for him. Come on, Con," Billy pleaded. "Let's think about reality here. You know that it's in our best interests not to fall behind schedule any more than we already have," he added pointedly.

Connor was silent for a long moment. Joe began to fidget. *They haven't even asked me if I'm interested in taking the role,* he thought. *But it would be cool to be in a movie, although I'm pretty busy with my summer job at the bookstore.*

Wishbone came running up to Joe just then. He rubbed up against his pal's leg.

"Hi, boy," Joe said. He reached down to scratch Wishbone's ears. He felt a bit awkward and out of place—surrounded by the Drake brothers, and all these actors and crew members. It was nice to have his best buddy by his side.

Connor fixed his eyes on Joe again. "All right," he said with a sigh. "You've got the part—if you want it."

Joe wasn't sure, but to him it seemed Connor wasn't too happy about the decision.

"Part? What part?" Sam had joined the group. She was putting the lens cap on her camera and stuffing a roll of exposed film into her pocket.

Joe started to tell her about the part of Byron Smith.

Before he got very far with his description, Sam cried out, "Joe! That's terrific! You're going to be in *Simon Moore!*"

"First, I have to ask Mr. Gurney if I can take time off from the bookstore—" Joe began.

"This would be for only one week, Joe," Billy cut in. "You're only in".—he paused to check the scene notes on his clipboard—"eight of the film's scenes," he finished.

Joe wanted to say that he would do his best in playing the part. But being the dinosaur in his school play didn't exactly qualify him to fill a role in a movie. What if he forgot his lines? What if he froze in front of the camera? *These guys should hire a real actor,* he thought. *But I guess they don't have the time or the money.*

Wishbone was looking up at Joe. It was strange,

but Joe felt as though his dog was trying to tell him something. "Go ahead," Wishbone seemed to be saying. "You can do it!"

"Go for it, Joe," Sam said enthusiastically. "You may never have another chance like this."

Joe glanced toward Connor and Billy, and he took a deep breath. "I'll do it," he blurted out. "But I have to get permission first from my mom, and from the man who owns the bookstore where I have my summer job."

"That's fine, Joe," Connor said. "As long as you speak to them quickly. We'll need you for your first scene tomorrow morning—"

"Bright and early," Billy added. "Welcome aboard, Joe Talbot!"

Sam smiled, and Wishbone began to bark and do backflips. Joe felt dazed and happy and uneasy, all at the same time. *I'm going to be in a movie,* he told himself. *I'm going to be in a movie.* It didn't seem real.

Chapter Three

Through an open window in his bedroom, Joe could hear the sound of crickets chirping. He could also feel just a hint of a summer breeze. He glanced at the clock near the edge of his nightstand; it was almost ten P.M.

Yawning a little, Joe leaned back against his pillow and closed the *Simon Moore* script. Connor had given it to him so he could get a head start on learning his lines. It was the third time he had read it that evening. Wishbone was on the bed, too, curled up in his usual place, near Joe's feet, and snoring softly.

Joe had to admit that the *Simon Moore* story was good. Simon Moore had been a real person living in Oakdale in the 1880s. When he was only eighteen years old, a group of dishonest and dangerous men decided to have him elected mayor so they could use him for their own selfish purposes. They conned him into doing lots of shady business deals in order to make themselves rich. But eventually, Simon caught on to their trickery.

Then the men tried to get Simon to approve the construction of a smoke-belching, noisy factory right in the middle of a park. He did not approve of this factory. Simon then found himself faced with a difficult decision: He had to either stand up and disagree with the men and possibly risk his life, or he had to join together with them and risk losing his honor—as well as destroying the future of Oakdale.

Joe opened the script to the last page and frowned. The strange thing was, the final scene was missing. So Joe had no idea how the story would end—or what Simon eventually decided. "Maybe this is a defective copy or something," he told himself. "I'll get a new script from Billy tomorrow."

Just then, his mom poked her head in the door. "Are you asleep, Joe?"

Joe smiled and shook his head. "Asleep? No way, Mom. I'm too pumped up."

Ellen came into the room and sat down on the bed. She was tall and slender, with shoulder-length brown hair and dark brown eyes that were a lot like Joe's. "I still can't believe you're going to be in a movie," she said, folding her hands on her lap. "I'm so happy for you, Joe. So is Wanda—she called earlier, while you were out. She wants to interview you at some point for a feature article that she's writing for the *Chronicle*."

"I'm just glad Mr. Gurney gave me the week off," Joe said. "He was really nice when I talked to him on the phone. He said business has been a little slow at the bookstore, anyway."

Wishbone let out a huge yawn at that moment,

then rolled over and went back to sleep. Joe reached forward to give him a gentle pat.

"So tell me more about your part," Ellen said. "You're the son of the local butcher, right?"

"Right. I help out my dad with deliveries and stuff. In tomorrow's scene, I'm going to help him make a delivery to the mayor's house." Joe flipped through the pages to the beginning of Scene Four. "While I'm there, I overhear a bunch of men planning to get this young guy Simon Moore elected mayor so they can take advantage of him," he added, his fingers trailing down the page.

Ellen steepled her hands together under her chin. She seemed to be considering something. "The whole thing takes place in the 1880s, right?" she said after a moment.

Joe nodded. "Right. Everyone wears these old-fashioned costumes, and they travel by horse-drawn carriages. And you won't believe this—the pork chops at Smith's Butcher Shop cost five cents apiece!"

"Wow—prices *have* gone up in the last hundred years," Ellen joked. Then she rose to her feet. "Listen, I have an idea. I'll be right back."

While his mom was gone, Joe turned his attention back to Scene Four of the script. He recited his lines to himself a few more times. Finally, he was convinced that he had them down perfect.

"Piece of cake," he said to himself. But deep down, he knew that tomorrow would be a different ball game. It was one thing to run through his lines in his room with no one around. It was another thing altogether to say them convincingly and realistically in front of a camera, with lots of people watching and listening. Also, Connor would be there, supervising like a hawk. And Joe had already seen what happened to the director's temper when filming didn't go just right.

When Ellen came back, she had a book in her hand. It was a big, fat paperback with an old-fashioned-looking photograph of a city on the cover.

"What's that, Mom?" Joe asked, sitting up a little.

"It's a book called *Time and Again,* by Jack Finney," Ellen replied. "It's a mystery about a man who time-travels back to the 1880s. It's full of wonderful historical details about that period, like how people dressed and what they ate and how the buildings looked. I thought it might help you 'get into your role,' as they say in the movie business."

Joe took the book from his mom and turned it over in his hand. Then he leafed through the pages. There were dozens of old-fashioned-looking photographs inside. There was even a picture of a horse-drawn

carriage like the one he, Sam, and Wishbone had seen on Main Street that afternoon.

"This looks like a great book," Joe said. "Did you say it was a mystery? Is it from . . . ?"

"Your dad's special box," Ellen said with a smile. "He enjoyed the historical side of the story. He also liked the fact that it was a morality tale of sorts—the hero has to dig down deep into his conscience to make some really tough choices about what is right and wrong in life," she explained.

Kind of like what happens in Simon Moore, Joe thought. "Thanks, Mom. I can't wait to read it."

After a few minutes, Ellen said good-night and left Joe's room. Joe set the *Simon Moore* script aside. He scrunched down under a thin cotton blanket and opened *Time and Again* to the first page. He knew it was late and that he should go to sleep. In fact, he couldn't seem to stop yawning suddenly. But he was really curious about this mystery story his dad had loved.

Joe's dad had died of a rare blood disorder when Joe was just six years old. Joe remembered playing catch with him, and watching him coach basketball at Oakdale College, and taking long walks with him through Jackson Park.

Joe had discovered a box of his dad's mystery books up in the attic. He had been reading them one by one: stories by great authors like Agatha Christie, Arthur Conan Doyle, Dashiell Hammett, and others. Now, he had a new one to dig into, by an author he had never read before. He grinned, wondering what his dad felt when *he* had first opened *Time and Again*.

Joe spent the next half-hour reading the first

chapters. The story immediately gripped his attention—and it seemed familiar, too. The hero, Si Morley, was working at his job at an advertising agency in New York when he was contacted by a college friend from his past. The buddy, Ruben Prien, told him that he wanted to hire Si for a top-secret government job. The job involved dressing up in 1880s clothes and acting like an 1880s person—and then, eventually, time-traveling from the present back to the 1880s. The thing was, Si wasn't sure why the government wanted him to do this, and the government wasn't very eager to explain.

For a moment, Joe's mind flashed to the *Simon Moore* set. He thought about the strange things that had gone on there earlier in the day: Connor's outburst; the odd conversation between the two brothers about some phone call and a woman named "Mrs. Crabbe." *Was there a mystery happening there, too?* Joe wondered.

He fell asleep before he could answer that question. The light on his nightstand was still on, his dad's copy of *Time and Again* was still propped open on his chest, and Wishbone was snoring softly at his feet.

Chapter Four

"Come on, Wishbone—there's our ride to the movie set!"

Wishbone stirred and opened one eye just a crack. He saw Joe standing in the hallway outside his bedroom, motioning for him to hurry up. His pal was dressed in jeans, layered shirts, and he had a backpack slung over one shoulder. His hair was still damp from his shower.

Very slowly and carefully, Wishbone opened his other eye. Joe went downstairs, followed by the sleepy Wishbone. The hall light was on. One of the living room lights was on, too. Wishbone went to his red chair in the study. He lay down and closed his eyes. He could smell coffee brewing in the kitchen and could hear the gurgling sounds of the coffee maker. Wishbone could also hear Ellen shuffling in her slippers from the refrigerator to the table and back again.

What is wrong with this picture? Wishbone asked himself. Shaking his head to clear some of the cobwebs, he peered sleepily at a window. It was still dark outside.

"Uh . . . Joe?" he said. "I don't know why you and Ellen are acting as if it's a fine Monday morning, because it's not. It's *nighttime.* And nighttime is when I do some of my best sleeping." He yawned and added, "I think you guys have me mixed up with a cat."

Wishbone closed his eyes and snuggled into a comfortable position. Just at that moment, he heard the unpleasant *beep!* of a car horn. *"Whassat?"* he cried out, jumping.

"Wishbone!" Joe said, more insistently this time. "If you don't wake up right now, our driver is going to leave without us!"

"Oh, well, I guess I can't get out of this one." Wishbone rose to all fours, stretched, and leaped down onto the floor. Yawning, he trotted into the kitchen to his food bowl. "I'll have to have my breakfast first, though, buddy. I can't go anywhere on an empty stomach."

"I've got your breakfast kibble in my backpack. You'll have to wait until we get to the set," Joe said, seeing Wishbone reach his empty food bowl.

"Wait? What? Joe, you can't do this to me!" Wishbone objected.

Joe said good-bye to his mom and opened the front door, heading outside.

Sighing, Wishbone followed him. "This is your big day, Joe, so I'm willing to make some sacrifices. But I expect lots of extra kibble when we get to the set."

Outside, the sky was black with a faint stripe of gray across the horizon. As Wishbone crossed the yard, he enjoyed the feeling of having his paws against the

soft earth and dewy grass. He was tempted to stop for an early morning dig, but he knew there wasn't time. "I'll have to catch you later, dirt!" he called out with a friendly wag of his tail.

The car was parked in the street, its engine idling. It was old and brown and badly dented, and it seemed to need a new muffler. Joe opened the door, and Wishbone hopped in.

The driver turned around. She was a middle-aged woman with glasses. She was wearing a *Simon Moore* baseball cap.

"Hi, Joe," she said cheerfully. "I'm Mrs. Drake, Connor and Billy's mom. What a cute dog," she added, smiling at Wishbone.

"Joe, I *like* this woman," Wishbone said, settling into the backseat.

Joe sat down next to him and closed the door.

Mrs. Drake shifted gears and started driving slowly down the street. "You're probably not used to getting up at four-thirty in the morning, are you, Joe?" she said after a moment.

"Four-thirty! No one told me it was four-thirty! Driver, turn this car around!" Wishbone exclaimed.

"I could hardly sleep last night, anyway," Joe admitted to Mrs. Drake. "I'm kind of nervous about being in front of the camera." He paused. "I've never done this kind of thing before."

"You'll do fine, dear," Mrs. Drake told him reassuringly. "Besides, Connor will work with you until you get everything right. He's a very patient director."

Patient? Wishbone thought. *Connor didn't seem very patient yesterday when he threw a tantrum and walked off the set. But maybe he had skipped lunch and was in a bad mood. That's the kind of thing that happens to me sometimes.*

Speaking of which . . . Wishbone could smell the familiar, meaty aroma of his kibble through the canvas material of Joe's backpack. His stomach grumbled.

"Uh . . . are we there yet?" he asked Mrs. Drake, who was making a left turn off Main Street. "We're talking emergency here—Code Blue."

"Here we are," Mrs. Drake sang out. She slowed down and pulled up in front of the warehouse. "Good luck, Joe. Nice meeting you, Wishbone. I'm sure I'll be seeing you both again."

Joe said good-bye to Mrs. Drake. Then he and Wishbone got out of the car. Wishbone glanced up and down the street. It was deserted at this hour, and kind of eerie. "Not a dog in sight," Wishbone said to himself.

Inside the warehouse, it was a different story. Like yesterday, it was a beehive of activity: crew members racing around, actors in costume running through their lines, equipment placed everywhere. Connor and Billy were sitting off in a corner drinking big cups of coffee. They were marking up what looked like a copy of the script.

"I'm ready for my close-up now, Mr. Spielberg," Wishbone called out to the brothers.

When they didn't reply, Wishbone peered up at Joe. He looked really nervous. He *smelled* nervous, too, Wishbone realized.

"Not to worry, Joe," he said, wagging his tail. "I'll be by your side the whole time, helping you with your lines—except for right now, when I'll be busy gobbling down my breakfast. Which brings me to my next point . . ."

"Joe!" Billy rose to his feet and waved at Joe with his coffee cup. "Good morning! Come on, let me show you around. I'll introduce you to some people."

"We'll be happy to meet everyone—*right after I've had my breakfast,*" Wishbone informed Billy. He sat down on his haunches next to Joe's feet. "Okay, Joe, I think this might be a good time to open up your backpack and serve up that yummy kibble. I'll take it over easy, sunny-side up, or scrambled . . . I'm not picky—especially at this time of day."

Instead of reaching into his backpack for the kibble, Joe went over to Billy. Connor said hello to Joe—without much enthusiasm, Wishbone thought—then wandered off to talk to a couple of actors.

Wishbone bounded after Joe. "Joe! Joe! Aren't you forgetting something?" he asked anxiously.

But by the time Wishbone reached Joe, his buddy was involved in a conversation with Billy. "After I show you around, we'll get you over to Makeup and Wardrobe," Billy was saying.

"Makeup?" Joe asked, frowning. "Like . . . uh . . . what kind of makeup?"

"Don't worry. We're not going to make you wear lipstick and eye shadow," Billy said, chuckling. "We're talking about a little foundation, a little powder—nothing too drastic. Hey, Leo!" he called out to a cast member who was walking by. "Come over here. There's someone I want you to meet before you head over to Wardrobe."

The person named Leo walked over. He was tall

and slender with curly, jet-black hair. He seemed to be in his late teens. He had a lean, handsome face and hazel eyes.

"Leo, meet Joe," Billy said. "Leo plays Simon Moore. Joe is our new Byron Smith."

"And I'm Wishbone, the cute little dog," Wishbone spoke up, wagging his tail politely. "The cute little *hungry* dog. Joe, are you catching any of this?"

"Leo Karras," Leo said, shaking Joe's hand. "K-A-R-R-A-S. I suppose you've heard of me." He smiled, showing two rows of perfect white teeth.

"Uh . . . well . . . I'm not sure," Joe said, frowning. "I guess your name *is* kind of familiar."

"Space Spuds," Leo said grandly. "A movie about giant mutant potatoes from outer space. I played Thor, the teenage alien warrior who saves the people of Earth from doom and destruction." He fixed his hazel eyes on Joe. "Don't tell me you didn't see it! For a while, it was playing every Saturday at three A.M., on cable TV."

"Sorry," Joe said apologetically. "But I'll look for it on video," he added.

Billy then introduced Joe to Fitch Carew, who was playing Byron Smith's dad, Beau Smith. Fitch was a heavyset man with thinning grayish-brown hair, friendly blue eyes, and a thick English accent. Billy also introduced Joe to Bert Guthrie, whom he referred to as the "D.P."

"D.P.?" Wishbone cocked his head. "Is that short for Dog Petter?"

"I'm the director of photography," Bert explained to Joe. "Also known as the cinematographer. And for this movie, I'm also the cameraman."

Fitch raised his hand in the air. "Listen, everybody, I have a question. Has anyone seen my costume for this scene? It is not in Wardrobe. I can't seem to locate it anywhere." He had a very formal way of speaking, which made him sound as though he were reciting lines from a Shakespeare play.

"The gray thing?" Billy shook his head. "I haven't seen it. Are you sure it's not in Wardrobe? Maybe it's hung up in the wrong place or something."

"The staff in Wardrobe said they double-checked, William. But I suppose I could check once more." Frowning, Fitch wandered off.

"I wish he'd stop calling me 'William,'" Billy said good-naturedly to Joe. He added, "By the way, I don't

know if I told you. I'm the child wrangler for this production, as well as the writer and A.D. That means I'm in charge of you."

"Child wrangler? That sounds kind of painful," Wishbone said worriedly. He lay down and listened as the conversation continued.

"Uh . . . I'm not sure I understand that term," Joe said politely to Billy.

"A child wrangler takes care of any kids on the set," Billy explained to Joe, who also looked a little worried. "Just think of me as a big brother, or something like that." He put his arm around Joe's shoulders. "Okay, now, I'm gonna take you over to Makeup and Wardrobe. After you're through there, you and I and the others will do a run-through of the scene, with blocking—going over where everyone stands, where they should look, and when and where they should move. . . ."

Wishbone sighed as Joe walked away with Billy. "I'm beginning to get the picture. I'm on my own for breakfast. I guess it's every dog for himself around this place."

He got up on all fours and began to trot around the stage set. His stomach was *really* grumbling now. Plus, he had to make sure not to get stepped on, because the crew didn't seem too aware of his presence. At one point, he even came close to being run over by someone moving a heavy camera on wheels.

Still, it was interesting for Wishbone to see all the movie equipment—even though it *did* remind him of his unpleasant experience playing Mr. MacPooch. He jumped on top of a snakelike pile of cables, then leaped

41

in the air to try to reach a boom—a microphone hanging off a long pole. He stopped to listen to two of the actors running through their lines.

"Mr. Finnegan, I find myself having to ask you a most awkward question," one of them said. "It has to do with your colleagues' plans for the upcoming election—"

"Mr. Bainbridge, that subject is not open for discussion," the other one cut in sharply. "In fact, you must never breathe a word about it again—to me or to anyone else. You could put yourself in serious danger."

"Bainbridge, I need to see more *hunger,*" Wishbone advised when the two actors paused to review their scripts. "And, Finnegan, you've really got to put more *meat* into that speech." The little dog cocked his head. *"Hunger? Meat?* That reminds me—*I . . . must . . . find . . . breakfast!"* He quickly trotted away.

Acting on a hunch, Wishbone crossed through the main part of the warehouse and entered a small room off to one side. There, his hunch paid off. Right near the doorway was the best piece of equipment of all: the craft-services table!

"Bingo!" Wishbone cried out. He raised his nose in the air and inhaled deeply. "Bagels! And doughnuts! They even have cherry danishes, my favorite . . . well, one of my favorites."

Just then, Wishbone was distracted by the sound of a quick movement behind him. He whirled around. A little dog darted across the room, crossed behind him, then disappeared through the doorway. And it wasn't just *any* little dog—it was another Jack Russell terrier!

"Who was *that?*" Wishbone asked. "I wonder why she didn't stop for a snack and a chat." His tail began to wag. "But I can't think about her now. *I . . . must . . . eat.*" He prepared to put his front paws on the food-filled table.

Then Wishbone was immediately distracted again by something else. In his crouched-down position, he could see something half-hidden under the table, something gray. It appeared to be an item of clothing.

Wishbone was really curious. What could it be? Forgetting about the bagels, doughnuts, and cherry danishes for a moment, he inched forward, clamped his teeth around the item, then dragged it out into the light.

Huh? Wishbone thought, as he studied the gray heap. He had a sudden, bad feeling in the pit of his stomach, and it wasn't due to hunger.

The thing looked like an actor's costume—and it looked as though it had been ripped to shreds.

Chapter Five

Wishbone sniffed at the shredded costume. "Hmm . . . it smells familiar," he said to himself. "There's something else familiar about it, too. Now, who was talking about a missing gray costume . . . ?"

"My costume! You little mongrel! What have you done?"

Startled, Wishbone turned around. Fitch Carew, the actor who played the father of Joe's character, was standing in the doorway. He looked very angry—the same way Wanda Gilmore did whenever she spotted Wishbone doing a creative rearrangement of her flower beds. Connor and Billy were standing behind Fitch, looking puzzled.

"This furry creature has chewed my costume to smithereens!" Fitch complained to the Drake brothers. "What kind of set do you run here, anyway? How can you allow wild animals to roam around and create such a mess?"

"Hey! Who are you calling a wild animal, buster?"

Wishbone answered. "I was just minding my own business, trying to make a really tough decision between a cream-filled doughnut and a cherry danish. Then I suddenly spotted your costume under the table. *I* was the one who found it and rescued it!" He added, "Besides, how do you know that other dog didn't do this? You know, the *other* cute little Jack Russell terrier."

Just then, Joe showed up. He had beige makeup on his face, and his hair was slicked back and shiny. He smelled sweet. "What's going on?" Joe asked everyone who had gathered around.

Wishbone trotted over to Joe and gazed up at him with his best "I didn't do it" look. "Don't forget, in America dogs are innocent until proven guilty," he reminded Joe.

"Joe, I'm afraid that your dog destroyed Fitch's costume," Connor said angrily.

Billy turned to his brother. "Come on, Con—let's not jump to conclusions here."

"Finally, the voice of reason speaks up," Wishbone said, wagging his tail.

Joe went over to where the costume lay on the ground and knelt down in front of it. He picked it up and turned it over in his hands. "Wishbone didn't do this," he said after a moment. "Look at the tear marks—they're straight and clean. Someone did this with a knife or something else sharp."

"Thank you, Joe!" Wishbone said, standing up on his hind legs and pawing the air. "I knew that if anyone could clear my name, it would be you!"

Connor knelt down beside Joe. He took the costume in his own hands and studied it closely. "You're right,

Joe," he said after a moment. "I'm . . . uh . . . sorry I accused your dog so quickly."

"Apology accepted," Wishbone said, getting down on all fours. "Of course, where I come from, it's not a *real* apology unless you offer a small token, too— say, something edible . . ."

"I do *not* understand," Fitch cut in. "What would cause someone to do such a terrible and senseless thing? Stephen spent days making this costume. As you can see, some of the detailing around the pockets was done by hand."

"Our schedule," Connor said suddenly, glancing at his watch. "Go ask Stephen if he can throw another one of these together as soon as possible," he ordered Billy. "No, don't ask him—*tell* him."

Billy glanced at his own watch. "We're scheduled to start shooting Scene Four in forty-five minutes. Stephen works fast, but not *that* fast." He reached out for the tattered costume. "Here, give me that thing. Let's see if Stephen is up to performing a miracle today."

Connor handed the costume to Billy. Just as he did, a piece of folded-up paper fluttered out of the creases and fell to the floor, next to where Wishbone was sitting.

Wishbone bent down toward the piece of paper, sniffing curiously. "Hmm . . . it looks like our culprit left a clue. Joe, we have a real mystery on our paws!"

Joe bent down and picked the paper up and unfolded it. "It's a note," he announced.

Wishbone could see that the note was written in bright green ink.

"What does it say?" Connor asked Joe.

Joe stood up slowly. Wishbone could see that his buddy was frowning. *Uh-oh, it's something bad,* he thought. *Maybe it's a squeaky-toy recall. Or maybe Pepper Pete's is closing for repairs.*

Joe cleared his throat and read the note: "'If the past is changed, this film will never be made.'"

Joe read the note again, wondering what it meant. Was someone trying to keep *Simon Moore* from getting made? And what was this remark about the past not being changed?

Joe glanced up from the note, full of questions. But Fitch seemed to have wandered off somewhere, and Billy and Connor were having another one of their whispered conversations off in the corner. Connor looked upset, and Billy seemed to be trying to calm him down. At one point, Joe thought he heard Billy mention the name "Lucinda Crabbe."

That's the woman they were talking about yesterday, after Connor almost canceled the production, Joe thought. *Who is she, anyway? Could she have anything to do with the note and the destroyed costume?*

Bert Guthrie—whom Joe remembered as the director of photography—came running in to Connor and Billy. "Uh . . . what's up?" he asked, frowning at one brother, then the other. "I thought we were going to go over the lighting ten minutes ago."

"Right. I'm sorry," Connor apologized. "We found Fitch's costume under the craft-services table, and it was completely destroyed. Obviously, this was some-body's idea of a joke."

"A joke?" Joe repeated, puzzled. This seemed much too serious to be a joke. "But—"

"But we can't waste any more time worrying about it," Billy cut in. "We have to get a new costume made, plus do some run-throughs of Scene Four. Joe, buddy, you'd better get back to Makeup right away." He squeezed Joe's shoulder and smiled. Then he, Connor, and Bert hurried out of the room, talking with great concern about something called a flicker generator.

Joe touched his face; it felt a little sticky. Then he turned and headed back toward Makeup, deep in thought. He wondered again about the destruction of the costume, and the strange note. Who was behind these things? Was it all just a joke, as Connor suggested, or was someone really trying to stop the production of *Simon Moore* before it had ever gotten started?

Chapter Six

"I think we're about ready," Connor announced to the cast and crew. "Everybody, please take your places!"

Joe glanced up from his copy of the script and took a deep breath. He had spent most of the last hour rehearsing his lines for what seemed like the hundredth time. Now, the moment had come for him to play the scene for real.

There had been yet another delay while Stephen Chudej from Wardrobe had sewn together a brand-new costume for Fitch. During that time, Connor and Billy had taken the actors through several run-throughs of the scene, complete with blocking.

Now, if I can just keep everything straight in my head! Joe thought nervously.

He glanced down at his own costume: a pair of brown cuffless pants with suspenders, a high-collared white shirt, and scruffy-looking brown lace-up boots. He touched the brown cap that covered his slicked-back hair.

Joe knew he looked just like one of the 1880s figures in the old photographs in his dad's book, *Time and Again*. The amazing thing was, he was beginning to *feel* like one of them, too. It was strange how wearing 1880s clothes could make him *feel* like an 1880s person.

Joe knew that Si Morley, in *Time and Again,* experienced that same feeling, too. When Si was preparing to go back in time, he did a "practice" run into a set made to look as if it were from the 1880s. He put on his "costume"—cuffless wool pants, a green-and-white-striped shirt with no collar, wide suspenders, and a double-breasted black vest with a gold watch chain slung across it.

Then Si walked into an apartment in New York City that had been furnished entirely in an 1880s style. Si knew that the twentieth century was just outside the closed drapes of his windows. But he really felt he was actually in the past—just by being in his old-fashioned outfit, and by being in this old-fashioned apartment.

Now, Joe felt the same way, too. He could easily imagine that he was a resident of long-ago Oakdale, in the time of his great-great-grandparents. Or was it his great-great-*great*-grandparents? He made a mental note to ask his mom later that night.

Just then, Wishbone came running up to Joe. His whiskers were covered with something gooey and white, as though he'd been eating some food that was cream-filled.

That reminded Joe. He hadn't fed Wishbone his breakfast. The kibble was still in his backpack.

"Sorry, boy," Joe said, patting the dog on the head. "I guess I forgot to feed you."

Joe took a closer look at Wishbone's muzzle. That definitely looked like cream.

"Well, it looks as if you found a substitute meal. Listen, as soon as we get a break from shooting, I will open up that kibble." Kneeling down, Joe scratched between Wishbone's ears. "We're about to start shooting, so you just stay on the sidelines, okay, boy?" he said.

In response, Wishbone licked Joe's hand—as if to wish him good luck. Then he trotted off to a corner and curled up on the floor. Joe grinned at his dog. It was really great to have his number-one fan on the set with him.

Billy lifted his walkie-talkie to his lips. He pressed a button, and it crackled to life. "I need the A-team in here, pronto!" he spoke into it. He smiled at Joe, gave him the thumbs-up sign, and mouthed the words: *You're gonna do great.*

Joe smiled back. *Billy's such a nice guy,* he thought. *I'm glad he's in charge of me, and not Connor.* He glanced at the director, who was barking orders at one of the crew members.

Just then, GiGi Coker—the makeup artist—came rushing up to Joe. "Touch-up," she said cheerfully. She lifted a fluffy brush to his face.

While GiGi refreshed Joe's makeup, he stood very still and took in the action all around him. Production was really getting under way now. Bert was standing behind the camera making some last-minute adjustments. The boom operator was holding the long microphone in the air to capture the actors' lines. The sound mixer was at the tape recorder, fiddling with the controls. And the lighting people were up on scaffolds, looking down on the action. More crew members were hurrying around with clipboards and cables. The actors in the scene were getting into position.

Joe knew that he—Byron Smith—would be going before the camera right at the beginning of the scene. Byron was to help his dad deliver some roasts to the mayor's mansion for a big political banquet.

"Joe, are you ready?" Billy's voice cut into Joe's thoughts. GiGi had gone off to powder someone else's nose.

Joe took a deep breath and nodded. "I'm ready . . . I *think*." One of the prop people handed him his prop for the scene: a big package wrapped in butcher's paper and tied up with string. Joe took it and tucked it under his arm.

Billy lifted the walkie-talkie to his lips. "We're going for picture. Lock it up!" he ordered.

Connor crossed his arms over his chest and cleared his throat. Everyone on the set fell silent. "I know we're going to nail this scene very quickly," he said. "I have tremendous faith in all of you." He turned to his brother and said, "Go ahead and call it, Billy."

Joe had no idea what the brothers were talking about. "Locking it up" and "calling it" were terms he had never heard of. But he didn't have time to ask anyone what they meant. Everything was happening really fast.

"Roll sound!" Billy instructed.

"Speed!" the sound mixer replied.

"Roll camera!" Billy told Bert.

"Rolling!" Bert replied.

A young woman held up something Billy had

referred to earlier as a "slate." It was a small black-and-white board—like a miniature blackboard—with a bunch of words written on it: *Simon Moore,* Connor and Bert's names, the date, and "Scene 4, Take 1." The woman lifted the top part of the slate—a long, skinny wooden bar—and slapped it down quickly with a loud *clack.*

"Scene Four, Take One!" she called out loudly.

Connor leaned forward and raised his hand in the air. "Everybody settle . . . and . . . *action!*" He then turned to Joe and nodded.

I'm on! Joe thought. He felt excited and nervous, the same as when it was the last few seconds of a big basketball game, his team was down by two points, and he had the ball in his hands. *Okay, Talbot, you can do this,* he told himself.

Trying to ignore the pounding beat of his heart—and the fact that dozens of pairs of eyes were on him—Joe adjusted the package in his arms and walked through a fake door that was part of the set. He entered the lavishly furnished hallway that was supposed to be part of the mayor's house. Suddenly, he thought of *Time and Again.* The story flickered briefly through his mind. Like Si Morley, Joe was leaving the twentieth century behind and entering the 1880s. . . .

Whistling softly, just as Connor had instructed him to do, Joe walked down the hallway. After a moment, he reached his mark—a small piece of white tape that had been placed on the rug for his benefit so he would know exactly what his physical position was supposed to be—and stopped.

The script called for Byron to be looking for his father, so Joe quickly looked around. . . .

Joe continued to walk down the hall. *So far, so good,* he told himself. When he came to a brown door, he paused—just as Connor had told him to do—and peeked inside. He started to open the door.

Then Joe hesitated. On the other side of the door was a parlor. Inside, two actors dressed in elegant-looking suits were talking.

"Mr. Finnegan, I find myself having to ask you a most awkward question," one of them said. "It has to do with your colleagues' plans for the upcoming election—"

"Mr. Bainbridge, that subject is not open for discussion," the other cut in. "In fact, you must never breathe a word about it again—to me or to anyone else. You could put yourself in serious danger."

"Danger? But I don't understand." The first actor glanced around nervously.

There was a long pause. "Just between you and me, Mr. Bainbridge, my men plan to see that our candidate is elected—no matter what it takes," the other actor said at last.

"Your candidate? And who would that be?"

"His name is Simon Moore."

The one playing Mr. Bainbridge gasped. "Simon Moore? You don't mean William Moore's son, do you? Why, he's still a child!"

The one playing Mr. Finnegan nodded. "Exactly."

Fitch should be coming down the hall about now, Joe thought. Then, right on cue, Joe heard Fitch's heavy footsteps approaching.

"Byron, ya fool, you're not supposed to be in this part of the house!" Fitch called out gruffly to Joe's character. "The kitchen is *that* way. The cook's waitin' for the roasts."

Joe was struck, as he had been during rehearsal, by the way Fitch was able to drop his normal thick English accent and speak in a different accent altogether. *He's a pretty awesome actor,* Joe thought.

Joe turned to look at Fitch, as his father, who continued to walk toward him, and then at the two men in the parlor. They had fallen silent, and were crossing the room to see who was in the hallway. Joe was about to be discovered!

Fitch was almost at Joe's side now, wearing his newly sewn gray costume. "Next time you help me make a delivery, son, you stay by my side, do ya hear?" he said in a stern voice. "And furthermore— *Yow!*" Suddenly, Fitch tripped on a rug and tilted forward. Pulling back, he overcompensated and fell flat on his backside.

"Cut!" Connor yelled.

"That's a cut!" Billy said into his walkie-talkie. "Release the lockup and stand by."

All of a sudden, Joe was aware of the mood on the set changing, like a shifting of gears. People started rushing around again. There was suddenly all sorts of activity, all different sounds and voices. It was as though Joe—and everyone else—had been jolted back into the twentieth century with the word *cut!*

Connor was helping Fitch to his feet. "Are you okay?" the director asked, looking concerned.

Fitch rubbed his elbow. "Yes, I suppose so. Really, these prop people must be more careful about taping down the rugs."

Billy sighed and lifted the walkie-talkie to his lips again. "Props, we need some electrician's tape in here, please," he said. "Joe, you're doing great," he told Joe.

"Thanks," Joe said, grinning. He was really relieved that he had made it almost all the way through the scene. Of course, they would have to do another take now. And maybe another one after that . . .

Fitch continued to rub his elbow with his right hand. As Joe watched him, he noticed something peculiar. There was a bright green ink smudge on Fitch's hand.

Joe frowned. The note they had found with the destroyed costume had been written in the same color of green ink, he thought to himself. Could Fitch have written the note—and ruined his own costume, too? But why?

Chapter Seven

"I thought I would include these photos I took at the crafts fair in my sample case. And maybe the wide-angle ones I took of the . . . Joe, are you listening?" Sam said, a bit annoyed.

"Huh?" Joe said, glancing up from his plate. Sam was staring at him from across the table with a puzzled expression on her face.

The two of them were sitting in Pepper Pete's. They were sharing a banana-and-pineapple pizza, a new "special" that Sam's dad was trying out on his customers. Sam had asked Joe to meet her there for dinner so he could help her put together a sampling of photos she had taken. Sam needed the portfolio to compete in a local photography contest. Joe liked Pepper Pete's, which had comfortable booths, a really great jukebox, and interesting pizzas.

"You haven't heard a word I've said in the last ten minutes," Sam said. "What's wrong?"

"I'm sorry, Sam," he apologized. "It's just that

so much has happened today. I guess that I'm kind of distracted."

Sam took a sip of her soft drink. "I know. It must be pretty exciting, being in *Simon Moore.*"

Joe grinned and nodded. He knew Sam would understand. "It's really fun pretending to be someone from the 1880s," he explained. "And everyone on the set is so cool. There's GiGi, the makeup artist, and Stephen from Wardrobe. Bert's the D.P.—that's short for director of photography. Oh, yeah, and Billy is the child wrangler, which means that he's in charge of me. He's a really nice guy. You'd like him a lot. I don't know how he puts up with his cranky brother, Connor, though. . . ."

Joe couldn't seem to stop talking. Between bites of pizza, he told Sam all about his scene, which had taken all morning and most of the afternoon to shoot. He had stuck around to watch a part of Scene Five being shot, even though he wasn't in it. Scenes Six and Nine, which had been on today's call sheet, had gotten bumped to tomorrow. The long delay in starting Scene

Four, due to the incident with Fitch's costume, had held up the day's production schedule.

"The scenes are being shot out of order," Joe explained to Sam. "It all depends on what sets we have ready to use. For example, Scenes Four, Five, and Nine all take place in the mayor's mansion. So we're doing them pretty much together. Later on, we'll go back to Scene Three, which takes place outside."

Then Joe told Sam all about the ruined costume and the threatening note.

He added, "It's really strange. The green ink stain on Fitch's hand makes me think that he's the culprit. But why would he do that to his own costume? And what does he mean by saying if the past is changed, *Simon Moore* will never be made?"

"Sounds like a mystery to me," Sam remarked. She glanced down at her pile of photographs, fingered a few of them, and fell silent.

"And speaking of mysteries . . . I'm reading this book from my dad's box," Joe continued, reaching into his backpack. "It's called *Time and Again.*" He quickly summed up the plot for Sam and added, "I'm at this part where Si Morley goes back to the 1880s. And this time, he's really time-traveling, not just pretending."

Sam looked interested. "How does he do *that?*"

"At first, Si dresses up in 1880s clothes and lives in an 1880s apartment and just pretends to go back in time," Joe explained. "But after doing this for a few days, one of the men from the government hypnotizes him. Then Si travels back in time for real."

Sam frowned. "You mean, he gets *hypnotized* into thinking he goes back in time for real?"

Joe shook his head. "Nope. The hypnosis just makes it a little easier to do the time-travel. He really does go back in time, like in a science fiction movie." He added, "Anyway, Si's supposed to be observing what life was like back then as part of his top-secret job. But he also has a mission of his own—he wants to see who mails a certain letter from a certain post office on January 23, 1882."

"Why?" Sam asked curiously.

"This letter was sent to the grandfather of Si's girlfriend," Joe explained. "And the grandfather committed suicide years later because of something that was in the letter. So Si's girlfriend wants him to find out who mailed it. She thinks it will help her understand why her grandfather killed himself."

Sam whistled. "Wow! That sounds like quite a complicated plot."

"It gets even better," Joe went on. "The letter was partially burned at some point, so there are a bunch of words missing. So it doesn't make sense to anyone."

"A mysterious letter that doesn't make sense," Sam remarked. "Sounds familiar, huh?"

Joe took another bite of pizza and nodded eagerly. "Yes, it does. Now, I'll just have to keep reading *Time and Again* to see how Si Morley solves *his* mystery. Then maybe I can solve the one that's happening on the *Simon Moore* set."

"Hi, Joe and Sam!"

They glanced up. Wanda was walking toward them, waving a folded-up newspaper in her hand. She was dressed in a sundress with poodles all over it. She wore red high-top sneakers on her feet.

Wanda set the newspaper down on their table with a *thump.* "Did you read my story? It's titled 'Oakdale Welcomes *Simon Moore* Cast and Crew!'" She unfolded the paper, revealing the blazing headline.

Joe leaned forward to read it. There was Wanda's article right on the front page, along with a photograph of the horse-drawn carriage that they had seen yesterday. There were some photos of the set, too, and individual head shots of Billy, Connor, and Leo.

Joe and Sam scanned the article quickly. Wanda had written about the history of the film project. She gave brief biographies of the primary cast and crew members. The story also quoted the reactions of local residents to the whole *Simon Moore* event.

Wanda also discussed the difference between making low-budget, independent films like *Simon Moore,* and big-budget Hollywood films. Joe read that part with interest:

> With a low-budget, independent film, money is always an issue, and the producer must make use of clever ways to cut corners as much as possible. In *Simon Moore,* many of the actors are amateurs, as well as being locals. They are working for little or no money.
>
> Additionally, many of the crew members are wearing more than one hat. For example, Billy Drake, the scriptwriter, is also the assistant director and child wrangler.

"It's a terrific story," Sam told Wanda. "Great photos, too."

"Why, thank you, Sam," Wanda replied, beaming.

"It says here that Connor and Billy grew up in Oakdale," Joe said, pointing to the last paragraph of the piece. "Did you know them, Miss Gilmore? I mean, before they went off to college and film school."

Wanda nodded. "I certainly did. They are Jim and Joanna Drake's boys."

Joe realized that Joanna Drake was the woman who'd driven him and Wishbone to the set early that morning.

"I would see Connor and Billy in Jackson Park from time to time," Wanda went on. "Connor always bossed Billy around, but Billy worshipped him. It seemed that no matter how demanding Connor was to Billy, Billy would do anything for Connor."

Joe was thoughtful. *Connor and Billy are still like that,* he thought. *Connor bosses Billy around, but Billy's always cheerful and good-natured about it. I wonder if Billy ever gets tired of being treated like that.*

Late that evening, Joe lay back on the living room couch and read more of *Time and Again*. Wishbone was curled up beside him, half-asleep. Joe absentmindedly scratched Wishbone's ears as he read. The movement made the little dog's tail thump rhythmically against the cushion.

In this part of *Time and Again,* Si Morley was back in 1880s New York City, taking in the sight of Fifth Avenue as it had been more than a hundred years ago.

Gone were the Empire State Building and Rockefeller Center and all the other high-rises. Gone were Saks Fifth Avenue, Tiffany's, and the rest of the fancy department stores. Instead, Fifth Avenue was a narrow, cobblestoned street lined with modest brownstones—flat-roofed houses made of reddish-brown stone. Instead of a sea of taxicabs with blaring horns, a few horse-drawn wooden buses clattered by quietly.

Just then, Ellen came into the living room. She was wearing a blue terry-cloth robe, and she had a book tucked under her arm.

"Hi, Joe," she said, perching on the edge of the couch. "How are you enjoying *Time and Again?*"

"It's great," Joe replied. "I wish I could stay up all night reading it, but I've got to be at the set early tomorrow morning."

"You certainly are busy," Ellen remarked. "By the way, I almost forgot to tell you. David called twice this afternoon. He and his family are back from their camping vacation. He seems very eager to tell you all about it." Besides Sam, David Barnes was Joe's other best friend, and next door neighbor.

"I'll call him tomorrow," Joe said, a little bit disinterested. Normally, he would have gotten up and phoned David right then and there. But he really wanted to get back to *Time and Again.* He also wanted to run through his lines for tomorrow's scene before going to bed.

Ellen gazed at Joe for a moment. Then she patted his knee and got up. "Well, I'm going to go upstairs and do some reading myself," she said. "Good night. Don't work too hard."

Joe smiled at her. "Good night, Mom."

Still curled up at Joe's side, Wishbone let out a big snore. Joe chuckled softly, then turned his attention back to his book.

Back again in the present day, Si was talking to his friend Ruben Prien and the other government officials who had hired him. They were pleased with his reports about what society was like during the 1880s. Si had successfully gone into the past without changing history in the least. They warned him that he had to continue to be extremely careful on his time-travel trips. He had to remain a fly on the wall, a twig in the river, an invisible observer.

Joe glanced up and stared thoughtfully out the window. He gave some consideration to the mysterious note in bright green ink. That, too, had to do with not changing the past.

If the past is changed, this film will never be made.

What did the message mean? It was one thing for Si Morley, a fictional character, to go back in time and tamper with historical events. But how could anyone involved with *Simon Moore* do the same?

Chapter Eight

Wishbone yawned and opened his eyes. This Tuesday morning the set was buzzing with activity, as usual. That was fine with the little terrier, as long as no one made him move from his cozy spot on the director's chair.

"It looks as if Joe's still in Makeup, getting ready for his next scene," Wishbone told himself. "That means I can squeeze in another short nap before I have to give him his pep talk. I think he's doing really well so far in his film role."

He snuggled into a more comfortable position and released another really big yawn. He still hadn't adjusted to this crazy, up-before-dawn schedule. *No wonder cats are so strange,* he thought. *It's not natural to start your day before the day actually starts!*

Still, Joe seemed to have adjusted just fine. Riding his bike to the warehouse this morning, Joe had run through his lines several times, and he hadn't seemed tired or nervous at all.

That's my boy, Wishbone thought proudly. *I trained him really well.*

Joe's scene this morning was to take place in Smith's Butcher Shop, which belonged to Fitch's character, Beau Smith. A couple of scary men were going to pay Fitch a visit to discuss what his son— Byron, played by Joe—may or may not have overheard at the mayor's mansion the day before.

Hmm . . . butcher shop, Wishbone thought, as his eyelids fluttered shut. *I wonder if they'll be using real meat for props. T-bone steaks . . . pork chops . . .* He yawned again.

Then Wishbone was distracted from his sleepy thoughts by an interesting sound: nails clicking on the warehouse's cement floor. His ears perked up, and his eyes snapped open.

And then he saw her. It was the cute little Jack Russell terrier from yesterday! She was walking across the set, accompanied by a woman with short brown hair and glasses.

Without wasting a second, Wishbone went trotting over to the other dog. She was even cuter up close. *In fact,* Wishbone thought, his heart beating a little faster, *she's about the cutest dog I've ever seen!*

"Hey, there!" Wishbone called out to her. "Wait up! I didn't get your name the other day. You want to go dig together or something?"

The dog paused in her tracks and glanced at Wishbone. She cocked her head, let her tongue hang out, and panted a little.

Wishbone stopped in front of her and began to sniff, to show that he was friendly. He gazed into her

big brown eyes, which were the beautiful color of mud puddles. "Hi. My name's Wishbone. What's yours?"

The other dog didn't reply.

"You're shy, huh?" Wishbone went on. "That's okay. I'm here with Joe Talbot. You know—tall, dark-haired, leading-man type. He's playing Byron Smith. Hey, you want to check out the craft-services table? I heard they've got blueberry muffins today." He added, "Maybe afterward, we could run around Jackson Park together. Or maybe I could show you some of my favorite spots in Wanda Gilmore's garden. . . ."

Just then, the woman with the glasses turned around. "Phoebe! Phoebe, honey, let's get you brushed before your scene!"

"Your scene?" Wishbone repeated, startled. "You mean . . . Hey! Are you in *Simon Moore*?"

Phoebe didn't say anything.

"Wow! You poor thing," Wishbone said. "Is this your first movie? Listen, let me give you the scoop on this business. You've heard of Mr. MacPooch, right? Well, I *was* Mr. MacPooch once—for a day. . . . Okay, it was more like a couple of hours. Anyway, being a canine superstar is no picnic. They make you wear these embarrassing costumes and pretend to talk— stuff like that. And the pressure! Everyone's constantly watching you, ordering you around. . . ."

The dark-haired woman called out to Phoebe again. "Come on, honey, we have to go!" She reached into her pocket and dangled a doggie biscuit.

Phoebe smiled shyly at Wishbone, then went running up to the woman.

"We'll talk later, okay, Pheebs?" Wishbone called after her. "I'll teach you the ropes, help you out with your lines, make sure that you're treated well. We dogs have to stick together!" He cocked his head and added, "Speaking of which, do you think you might talk your friend into giving *me* one of those biscuits?"

To Wishbone's surprise, Phoebe came trotting back to him. She dropped her biscuit in front of him and blinked her big, mud-puddle-colored eyes at him. Then she left the warehouse with the woman, glancing back one last time as she did so.

"Phoebe! Hey, Phoebe!" Wishbone called after her. He stared down at the biscuit, which lay on the floor in front of him. "I don't believe it. She gave me her biscuit . . . just like that. She's not only the cutest dog I've ever met, but she's the nicest, too."

Wishbone sighed happily.

"Wow! I think I'm in love." He picked up the biscuit with his teeth and quickly devoured it.

"You know, there's a positive side to the destruction

of Fitch's costume and the weird note about the past," Leo Karras said to Joe. "Publicity—with a capital P. This is a low-budget film, and it needs all the press coverage it can get. Otherwise, no one's going to come and see it. You following me, Joseph?" He flashed his pearly-white teeth at Joe.

Joe and Leo were sitting in Makeup, getting prepared for Scene Six. In this scene, Joe was going to watch from a back room in his dad's butcher shop as Mr. Finnegan and Mr. Bainbridge paid Beau Smith a visit. The two men were going to try to find out what Byron might have overheard about their plot to rig the election in order to get Simon Moore voted in. Halfway through the scene, Simon Moore—played by Leo Karras—was going to walk into the shop.

"Joe, sweetie, I need you to look to the left for a moment," GiGi said as she dipped a sponge into a big jar of beige foundation.

Joe did as GiGi asked. GiGi touched the sponge to his cheek; it felt cold and clammy, and he winced slightly.

"But if people read that there are problems on the *Simon Moore* set, why would that make them want to come and see the movie?" Joe asked Leo, puzzled.

"I've got to get more sponges. I'll be right back," GiGi announced.

"'Mystery on the *Simon Moore* Set'—people love that kind of a headline," Leo told Joe. He glanced in the mirror, tightened all the muscles in his face, then relaxed them. "It's a yoga exercise, to release tension," he explained to Joe. "You should try it sometime. *Anyway,* as I was saying, when the papers get wind of this mystery, they're going to eat it up. And all that publicity is going to create a lot of interest in the movie—which means interest in *me*." He added, "My agent says that if this movie does well, it could drive my career into high gear and launch me into superstar status."

"Wow! You have an agent?" Joe said, impressed.

Leo shrugged. "Sure. Don't you?"

"Uh . . . no," Joe replied. "I'm not really an actor. I'm just filling in for that guy who decided to drop out." He added, "So who do you think is responsible for the detroyed costume and the strange note?"

Leo suddenly looked distracted. "Uh . . . ah . . . who knows?" he mumbled.

Just then, Fitch Carew popped his head into the dressing room. "Excuse me, gentlemen, but by any chance do either of you know of Connor's whereabouts?" he called out.

"Nope," Leo replied. "He's probably on the set yelling at somebody."

Staring at Fitch, Joe thought once more about the green ink stain. He hadn't had a chance to follow up on that lead since discovering it yesterday.

"Oh, Fitch," Joe called out quickly as the actor turned to go. "Leo and I were just talking about what happened to your costume yesterday. Any idea who's responsible?"

Fitch stopped in his tracks. "I haven't a clue, my boy," he said slowly. "But if and when I catch the evil rascal, I will make him pay—him or her." He narrowed his eyes dramatically, then left the room.

Joe thought about this. *Fitch doesn't seem as if he's*

hiding anything. On the other hand, he's a really good actor. Still, what motive could he have for trying to shut down production of Simon Moore?

After Fitch was gone, Leo leaned over to Joe and said, "So . . . I suppose you've heard all the gossip about the top-secret last scene?"

Joe asked, "The . . . the what?"

"Connor and Billy won't release it." Leo glanced in the mirror and scrunched up the muscles in his face again. "They won't even tell any of us what happens in the exciting last scene."

Joe was silent. *So it's not just a coincidence that the last scene is missing from my script,* he thought. *I wonder why Connor and Billy are keeping it a secret.*

"You have to admit, it's kind of weird," Leo said, relaxing his face. "I mean, this movie's based on something that really happened in Oakdale in the 1880s. So it's not as if Connor and Billy need to sit around and try to come up with a new ending or something."

Just then, Joe heard a commotion outside in the hallway. A group of people were talking heatedly about something.

"Now what?" Leo said, his hazel eyes shining. "More trouble on the set? I'm telling you, Joseph, when the papers get wind of this stuff . . ." His words trailed off as he got up from his chair and rushed into the hallway.

Without wasting a second, Joe followed him. Connor and Billy were there, along with the head props person. Joe recalled that his name was Tom Rutherford.

"We are going to start shooting this scene in

twenty minutes, and *we need those props!"* Connor was saying to Tom in a tight, angry voice.

"And I'm telling you, Connor, I can't find them *anywhere,"* Tom replied, waving his clipboard in the air. "They were in the prop room last night. Now they are nowhere to be found. That can mean only one thing—somebody *stole* them!"

Chapter Nine

"Joe! Oh, Joe, there you are, buddy! I've been looking all over for you!" Wishbone put his paws into high gear as he caught sight of his friend.

Joe was standing outside Makeup talking to Connor, Billy, the prop guy, Tom Rutherford, and Leo Karras, the actor who played Simon Moore.

Wishbone had met Leo the day before, during Joe's first morning on the set. And Wishbone really liked Tom, who had played tug-of-war with him earlier with an old velvet sash.

Wishbone parked himself by Joe's feet and gave each of the guys a friendly smile.

"Hey, no one told me there was a party going on. Did anyone remember to bring the cheese and crackers?" He turned to Joe. "Listen, pal, I know I told you I'd help you with your lines before your next scene, but I was wondering if you could manage without me. See, I met this cute little Jack Russell terrier named Phoebe, and I thought I'd kind of hang out with her for a while. . . ."

Joe didn't seem to be listening. Instead, he was paying close attention to something Connor, Billy, and Tom were discussing.

"What do you mean, someone stole the props?" Connor was barking at Tom. "How can that be?"

"I'm telling you, that's what must have happened," Tom replied. "I locked the cabinets myself last night. I asked my staff if they opened them between then and now. They said no, and I believe them."

"Do you think it was the same culprit who destroyed the costume?" Joe asked. "If so, then maybe it's time to call the police. . . ."

Wishbone saw Billy and Connor exchange a glance. *Hmm . . . they are worried,* the terrier thought. *Kind of like the way I get whenever the Talbot household runs out of ginger snaps.*

"No police," Connor said firmly. "We can handle this ourselves."

"But, Connor—" Billy began.

"No police!" Connor repeated. "We can't afford to have any negative publicity."

"Excuse me, but there's something I've got to take care of," Leo said suddenly, and he turned to go.

"Who needs the police when you've got an excellent detective right here on the set?" Wishbone said to the brothers. "I'm talking about me, of course. I'd be happy to get to the bottom of this mystery for you—for a modest fee of three new squeaky toys." He sat down on his haunches and cocked his head. "Okay, first of all, has anybody found any clues? Maybe another one of those strange notes written in bright green ink?"

Joe turned to Tom. "Did anyone leave a note where the props were?"

"Joe, here, is my assistant," Wishbone explained to everyone. "I taught him everything he knows."

Tom shook his head. "No note."

"Look, we don't have time to talk about notes and suspects and all that nonsense," Connor said with irritation. "We have a scene to shoot." He frowned at Tom. "Is there any way you can come up with some new props for this upcoming scene in the next, say, ten to fifteen minutes?"

Tom glanced at his clipboard. "Let's see—a roll of butcher's paper and string. I think we've got more of that lying around here somewhere. But the cash register and the meat cleaver . . . Oh, and then there are the fake chickens, too. . . ." He shook his head. "I don't know, Connor."

Just then, Wishbone got an idea. "See you later, guys!" he said. "I have a mission to accomplish."

He put his nose to the ground and headed down a hallway.

"To the scene of the crime!" he said. "If the thief made off with the props, then he, she, or it must have left a trail. And I'm just the dog to sniff it out!"

Wishbone headed into the prop area and began to sniff in earnest. He picked up all kinds of interesting scents: glue, paint, marking pens, old coffee, stale doughnut crumbs. He helped himself to a couple of the doughnut crumbs, then continued his investigation. *Hmm . . . nothing much to go on here,* he thought.

He decided to expand his search to include the rest of the warehouse. He knew it was a big area to cover, but Connor and Billy and the rest of the cast and crew were counting on him!

"Excuse me, coming through, excuse me," Wishbone said as he made his way through the set. He passed the man in charge of the camera, a boom operator, and half a dozen actors rehearsing. "You gotta put more *oomph* into that line!" he called out to one of them. "Your tie's crooked, pal!" he called out to another. It made him feel good to know that he was being such a help to everyone.

Wishbone continued to comb through the rest of the warehouse. As he made his progress, he picked up some more interesting scents—and more doughnut crumbs, too. Unfortunately, he found nothing that might lead him to the missing props. In the back of his mind, he kept thinking that he might run into the fair Phoebe, but she was nowhere to be seen.

Eventually, Wishbone ended up in a room in a far corner of the warehouse. The room looked like some sort of storage area. A number of set pieces were stacked against the wall. There were also tools lying around on the floor. The scents of sawdust and turpentine hung heavily in the air. A dim, bare lightbulb hung from a cord on the ceiling, and it cast an eerie glow on everything.

"This is kind of spooky," Wishbone said to himself. "Hello! Is there anyone here? Any humans? Dogs? I'd even settle for a cat!"

No one replied.

"Hmm . . . I guess I'm all alone here," Wishbone told himself. "But that's okay—we detectives work best when we're solo. In *Time and Again*, Si Morley is

usually alone when he follows Jake Pickering around New York City."

Wishbone's thoughts remained briefly on *Time and Again.* He knew Joe was reading it now, and that his dad had read it a long time ago.

Wishbone loved the part where Si went back in time to January 23, 1882, and spotted Jake Pickering mailing the mystery letter to Si's girlfriend's grandfather. Si knew that Pickering—and the letter—was somehow connected to the suicide. At one point, Si even sneaked into Pickering's office, so he could search through his private files for information. . . .

"It's just like the way *I'm* searching for the missing props right now," Wishbone told himself. He put his nose to the ground and began sniffing again. "Props! Oh, props, where are you?"

As he approached a doorway, Wishbone detected an interesting new smell. He stopped and raised his nose in the air. It smelled like chicken feathers!

After a moment, he realized that the smell was coming from a large trash bin in a corner of the storage room. He trotted over to it, got up on his hind legs, and peered inside.

"Bingo!" Wishbone said to himself excitedly as he surveyed the contents. "An old-fashioned-looking cash register, a meat cleaver, a roll of butcher's paper, string, and three fake chickens with real feathers attached!" He leaped up into the air and did a triumphant backflip. "Mission accomplished! Am I *good,* or what?"

Joe heard Wishbone barking from somewhere in the distance. He knew there was another Jack Russell on the set—a dog named Phoebe, who had a role in the production of *Simon Moore*. Joe was sure, though, that it wasn't Phoebe making all that noise. Joe quickly recognized Wishbone's bark.

"I wonder what's up with Wishbone," Joe said to himself.

He sighed and put his script down on a chair. He started for the far end of the warehouse, where the barking was coming from. Joe had been going through his lines for Scene Six. With the props for that scene missing, however, there was some question about whether the cast and crew would have to postpone shooting the scene until later in the day.

Joe had a theory that the theft of the props was probably in some way connected to the destruction of Fitch's costume and the note about changing the past. The question was: Who was responsible for what had happened? Was it Fitch, or the mysterious Mrs. Crabbe, or someone else altogether? Joe also remembered that a strange phone call from someone had spooked Billy and Connor. Could that be related somehow to all the other mysterious events?

After a few minutes, Joe located Wishbone in what was a small storage room. "What are you doing here, boy?" he asked the terrier, who was sitting near a large trash bin. "Why were you barking? Are you hurt or something?"

Wishbone ran over to Joe and licked his hand. Then he raced back to the trash bin and propped his front paws up on the side of it.

Curious, Joe went over to the trash bin and peered in. Among its contents were a cash register, a meat cleaver, a roll of butcher paper, some string, and a bunch of fake chickens.

Wishbone had located the missing props!

"Good boy, Wishbone!" Joe exclaimed. "You found the props! Wait until— Hey, what's this?" His gaze fell upon a crumpled-up piece of paper that was lying on top of the cash register.

Curious, he picked up the piece of paper and smoothed it out. It appeared to have been torn from a page of a script—in fact, it was from the *Simon Moore* script:

FINNEGAN: Have you reached your decision, yet, Simon?

SIMON: I've given the matter a great deal of thought. . . .

BAINBRIDGE: Spare us the details of your soul-searching, *Mayor* Moore. What'll it be?

SIMON: *(pause)* Gentlemen, I've decided to go ahead with the factory. In fact,

The rest of the page was torn away.

Joe frowned. He didn't recognize this dialogue, and he'd read and reread the *Simon Moore* script about a dozen times. *Something's not adding up here,* he thought.

Then the answer came to him. This must be a page from the last scene of *Simon Moore:* the top-secret final scene that Connor and Billy had yet to release; the scene that only *they* knew about.

Excited by his discovery, Joe turned the piece of paper over in his hands.

He caught his breath.

On the back of the page was a phone number—written in bright green ink!

Chapter Ten

"Roll sound!"

"Speed!"

"Roll camera!"

"Rolling!"

Wishbone sat up straight, with a grin on his face. His eyes and ears were alert as Billy called the roll. Thanks to his heroic discovery of the missing props, the Scene Six shoot was staying pretty much on schedule. Now, he could hang out on the sidelines and relax. His belly was full and satisfied from his recent food-hunting expedition at the craft-services table. There, he had enjoyed a different kind of roll: a cinnamon roll.

"Scene Six, Take One."

"Everybody settle . . . and . . . *action!*"

The scene began. The setting was Smith's Butcher Shop. The set construction crew had built an 1880s-style store interior with gleaming white walls, high tin ceilings, and a long wooden bench for the customers to sit on while their orders were being filled. There were hand-written signs taped to the walls advertising the day's specials: PORK CHOPS—5¢; SIDE OF BEEF—40¢; CHICKENS—10¢.

There was a large, ornately carved mirror along one side of the set, making the shop appear even bigger than it was.

Fitch, as Beau Smith, was standing behind the long marble butcher's counter. He was working hard preparing the feathery, fake chickens and humming softly to himself.

Just then, the shop door opened. A small bell jangled. Fitch stopped humming and glanced up with a friendly smile, expecting customers.

Instead, the actors who played Bainbridge and Finnegan walked in. They looked bigger and more threatening than usual in their ankle-length coats and high top hats. They had nasty-looking scowls pasted on their faces.

Wishbone couldn't help shiver at the sight of the pair, even though he knew they were just acting.

"Hello, Beau," the actor playing Bainbridge said coldly.

"We want to talk to you about your son, Byron," the actor playing Finnegan added.

Wishbone craned his neck. Joe, as Byron, was peering through a back doorway at his movie father and the two men. Byron wore a worried expression.

"Way to go, Joe!" the little dog cheered. "Great concentration! You're really in character!"

As the scene progressed, the two men tried to find out from Beau just how much his son overheard when he had made his delivery at the mayor's mansion. They even made threats to Beau about keeping his son

"quiet." Eventually, Beau called Byron to the front of the shop and made him talk to the two men.

"But I didn't hear anything, Pa," said Joe, as Byron. "I was just looking for the kitchen, so I could deliver the roasts to the cook. Just like you said . . ."

As the various actors said their lines, the crew member in charge of the boom microphone kept shifting it around above their heads. Wishbone had to fight off the desire to go leaping up in the air after it. "I'll catch you later, boom—after the scene's over," Wishbone said.

The front door of the shop opened again. Leo Karras walked in, with Phoebe trotting happily at his side. As Simon Moore, Leo was dressed in cuffless brown pants with suspenders, a collarless cotton shirt, and a brown cap.

"Come on, girl," Leo said to Phoebe. "Good afternoon," he called out cheerfully to Fitch. "Ma's sick, so I'm doing the shopping for her today. I hope you've got some nice pork chops for our dinner."

Wishbone sat up straight, his tail wagging wildly—and it wasn't just because Simon happened to mention pork chops. Phoebe was making her acting debut! Her spotted coat gleamed under the bright lights. It looked as though it had been brushed a hundred times. She glanced up at Simon with her beautiful mud-puddle-colored eyes and followed him obediently through the store.

"That's it, Pheebs!" Wishbone said, keeping his voice low so he would not disrupt the scene. "Go with the flow. Be in the moment. I know you're really nervous, but you can do it! I'll be coaching you every paw print of the way!"

Phoebe didn't seem to be listening to Wishbone. In fact, she didn't seem to be very nervous at all. As the scene progressed, Wishbone could see that she was very relaxed in her screen role. She even seemed to be having fun!

Wishbone also noticed that Phoebe wasn't wearing a costume, as he had to do when he played the part of Mr. MacPooch. She wasn't even wearing a hat or a bonnet, or one of those high Victorian-era collars that stuck out every which way and made it hard to move one's head.

"Hmm . . . maybe show business isn't as bad as I thought," Wishbone said. "Pheebs, here, seems to be having a great time!"

Ten takes later, Connor finally called a wrap for the scene. Phoebe immediately came trotting over to Wishbone. He was so happy that his tail went into a high-speed wag. She really *was* cute—and so sweet, too.

"Hi, Phoebe," Wishbone greeted her. "Great job! You should get an award for your work—you know, for Best Dog in a Supporting Role."

Phoebe put her furred face very close to Wishbone's. Then she licked him on the nose.

"Come on, Phoebe!" Her handler, Jackie Kaptan, was waving at her. "Time for your walk!"

Phoebe stared sadly at Wishbone. Then she turned to leave.

"That's okay, Phoebe," Wishbone called out to her. "We'll get together later, okay? We can take a moonlit stroll through Jackson Park, and maybe do some digging, too."

"Hi, Wishbone." Joe came up to him and

scratched him behind one ear. "Thanks for being so patient."

"Mmm . . . more to the left, Joe," Wishbone said, moving his head. "Good—*there!*" He added, "You did really nice work today, buddy. I think a celebration dog treat would be in order, don't you? Or, better yet, how about a celebration pizza? Nothing says 'It's a wrap!' better than a large pizza with extra pepperoni."

Billy passed by just then. His head was bent over his clipboard. He paused, glanced up, and grinned at Joe. "Good work," he said warmly.

Joe's face lit up. "Thanks a lot, Billy," he said.

Joe turned toward Wishbone. "I'll take you for a walk in just a minute, okay, boy?" Joe said to Wishbone when Billy had left. "But first, I have to find a pay phone."

Wishbone knew Joe was eager to call the mysterious phone number that they'd found on the crumpled-up piece of the *Simon Moore* script.

"Great idea, Joe," he said enthusiastically. "How about biking to Pepper Pete's? You can use the pay phone there. We're talking bike, walk, phone call, and celebration pizza all rolled up in one neat package. How can you say no to that?"

Late in the afternoon at Pepper Pete's, Joe dug through his pockets for a quarter. He had been waiting all morning to get to a pay phone so he could call the number he'd discovered at the warehouse.

He knew he should have told Connor or Billy

about the crumpled-up piece of script—especially Billy, whom he felt really comfortable talking to. But something had held him back. Maybe it was because of the way the brothers had not paid serious attention to the note they had found with Fitch's destroyed costume. They had referred to the whole episode as a "joke." Joe wanted to get some hard facts about this new clue before sharing the information with either Billy *or* Connor.

In the background, a rock-and-roll song was playing on Pepper Pete's jukebox. Joe hadn't meant to go all the way to Pepper Pete's just to use a phone. He'd really only wanted to bike down Main Street, use the pay phone on the corner, and let Wishbone get a little exercise.

But Wishbone had taken off as soon as they'd left the set and headed straight for the pizza parlor. So Joe had figured that he might as well take care of everything at one place—make his call, grab some lunch, and catch up with Sam, who was helping her dad with the late lunch crowd.

Joe glanced across the room toward his favorite booth. Wishbone was waiting patiently there for their double-pepperoni pizza.

Sam was serving the day's special—sausage with mushrooms and extra cheese—to a nearby table of cast and crew members from *Simon Moore*. Joe recognized Tom, the props coordinator; Bert, the D.P.; Leo; Fitch; and several others.

"Bingo!" Joe's fingers finally seized upon a quarter in his right front pocket. It was mixed in there among crumpled gum wrappers and a bunch of pennies. He pulled it out, inserted it into the pay phone, and dialed the phone number.

While waiting for an answer, Joe thought about the events of the last few days. First, someone had destroyed Fitch's costume and left a mysterious note in green ink, saying that *Simon Moore* would never be made if the past was changed. Then, today, someone—possibly the same person—had taken props for Scene Six and hidden them in an out-of-the-way place.

The bright green ink used on the note and also on the piece of script paper Joe was holding was identical. Evidence seemed to point to Fitch, who'd had the same color ink on his hand yesterday. But what motive could he possibly have for destroying his own costume—and the production as a whole?

There was something else bothering Joe, too. Who was this Mrs. Crabbe that Billy and Connor kept whispering about? *Maybe I should just come right out and ask Billy about her,* Joe thought. *But then again, I don't want him to think that I've been eavesdropping on him and Connor. . . .*

A female voice at the other end of the phone cut into Joe's thoughts. "Where *is* that driver . . . ? Hello?"

"Uh . . . hello," Joe replied, startled. Deep down, he hadn't actually expected anybody to answer. Briefly, he wondered if this might be Mrs. Crabbe.

Frowning, Joe thought quickly for something to say to the woman, whoever she was. This was like acting in a scene without a script, he thought. It was what Si Morley had done whenever he time-traveled back to the 1880s. Si always found himself making things up on the spur of the moment to convince the citizens of the 1880s that he was one of them.

Joe stepped to one side as a waitress rushed by with a tray of soft drinks. *Okay, Talbot, the clock's ticking,* he told himself. *What should I say to her? Should I just come right out and ask her if she knows who's trying to shut down the production of* Simon Moore?

"Hello? Are you still there?" the woman at the other end of the line demanded. "To whom am I speaking?" She sounded annoyed now.

There was something familiar about the woman's voice. *Where have I heard it before?* Joe wondered.

"This is . . . uh . . . Joe Talbot." *Brilliant! Now what?* "Uh . . . who is this?" he asked.

"This is Margaret Bradbury, of course," the woman snapped. "Joe Talbot—should I know you?"

Margaret Bradbury. Joe recognized the name right away. Ms. Bradbury worked for the Windom Foundation, which gave money to lots of local organizations. He knew from his mom that the foundation gave a lot of money to the Henderson Memorial Library every year. Joe also saw Ms. Bradbury on the news from time to time, being interviewed about various community issues and events.

Joe frowned at this puzzling new twist in the ever-widening mystery. Was it possible that Ms. Bradbury was involved in trying to destroy the *Simon Moore* production?

Chapter Eleven

Joe was confused. It seemed unlikely that someone like Ms. Bradbury, with such a fine reputation, would be involved in the production's destruction. On the other hand, Joe had found her home phone number among the stolen props and the film-script page.

Ms. Bradbury's voice cut into his thoughts. "Well, young man? I haven't got all day."

"I'm sorry, Ms. Bradbury," Joe apologized. "You don't know me, but I think you know my mom. Her name's Ellen Talbot. She works at the Oakdale library as a reference librarian."

Ms. Bradbury didn't reply.

Finally, Joe took a deep breath and blurted out, "Anyway, ma'am, I was . . . uh . . . wondering, if . . . uh . . . you happen to know a man by the name of Fitch Carew."

Joe wasn't sure where he was going with this line of questioning. But since Fitch was his top suspect at the moment, it made sense to try to find out if there might be a connection between him and Ms. Bradbury.

"Fitch Carew? You mean the history professor at Oakdale College?" Ms. Bradbury said impatiently.

Joe was caught off guard. He'd automatically assumed that Fitch was a professional actor. He had no idea that he was a history professor—and at Oakdale College, no less.

"To answer your question, young man—no, I don't know Fitch Carew personally," Ms. Bradbury went on. "So if that will be all, I have an extremely busy schedule."

"Right, Ms. Bradbury. Thank you for your time," Joe said.

After hanging up, Joe went to a booth and sat down. Wishbone sat across from him.

"Well, that was strange," Joe said.

Wishbone's tail thumped against the vinyl booth.

Joe glanced at Fitch, who was at a nearby booth with Leo and the others from the film set. Fitch noticed Joe and waved. Joe waved back, feeling all mixed up. He wasn't sure what to make of the information he had just learned from Ms. Bradbury.

The door to Pepper Pete's opened, and Wanda walked in. She glanced around, zeroed in on Joe and Wishbone, and made a beeline for their booth.

"Hi, Miss Gilmore," Joe said. Wishbone gave a short bark, as if to say hello, too.

"Hello, there, you two." Wanda slid into the booth across from Joe and leaned forward eagerly. "Joe, what do you know about some trouble that's been going on at the *Simon Moore* set?" she asked in a low voice.

Joe was taken by surprise. "Where did you hear about that?" he asked her.

"I got an anonymous phone call this morning from some person. I think it was a man, but his voice was heavily disguised." Wanda glanced over her shoulder, as if to make sure that no one was eavesdropping. "Anyway, this person said that the *Chronicle* might be interested in the fact that some real-life villain has been causing a lot of damage on the *Simon Moore* set."

Joe was silent as he listened to this information. Who could have tipped Wanda off? Was it one of the cast or crew, or someone not involved with the production? Could it have been the culprit himself—or herself?

Joe then recalled what Connor had said earlier in the morning, about not wanting any negative publicity surrounding the film. "I don't think I can talk about this, Miss Gilmore," he said after a moment. "I'm really sorry. You should go directly to Connor or Billy."

"I'll do that, Joe," Wanda said, patting his arm. "I respect your decision. But don't you worry. I have no plans to run some headline-screaming story about this culprit—if he even exists. *Simon Moore* is an important project for Oakdale. The last thing I want to do is to harm its success in any way."

Wanda got up to leave. Just then, Joe noticed that Leo was staring at her. Then Leo glanced briefly at Joe. He turned his gaze away quickly. Joe wondered what was going on with the young actor. Next to Leo, Fitch was carefully cutting up his pizza with a knife and fork.

A moment later, Sam came by with Joe's order. "One piping-hot double-pepperoni pizza for two," she said, smiling at Wishbone. Then she turned to Joe.

"Guess what, Joe. I got a call from someone at the Oakdale Historical Society this morning. It might use some of my photos of Oakdale College for its photography show in September!"

"That's great, Sam," Joe said, his mind elsewhere. Then he nodded his head at Fitch. "See that guy over there?" he asked in a low voice. "Him—the one in the denim shirt. That's Fitch Carew, who plays my dad, Beau Smith, in the movie. Did you know that he teaches history at Oakdale College?"

Sam frowned briefly at Joe. Then she turned to look at Fitch. Joe didn't know what Sam's frown meant, but he decided not to ask. *Maybe she's just having a bad day or something,* he thought.

"Now that you mention it, he does look kind of familiar," Sam said. She turned back to face Joe. "He's the one you were talking about last night, right? The one with the green ink stain on his hand?"

Joe nodded. He then brought Sam up to date on the

latest events: the stolen props, the phone number he found on back of the script page, his conversation with Ms. Bradbury, and his conversation with Miss Gilmore.

"I'm not sure how Ms. Bradbury is connected to all this—*if* she's connected at all," Joe concluded. "She said she didn't know Fitch personally." He took a bite of pizza and added, "I think it's interesting that Fitch is a history professor. I mean, think of what that note said: 'If the past is changed, this film will never be made.'"

Sam sat down next to Wishbone and scratched his ears. He made a satisfied noise. Then Sam pointed to Joe's copy of *Time and Again,* which was poking out of his backpack. "How's your book?" she asked Joe.

"Huh? Oh, that. It's good." Joe took a sip of his soft drink. "I'm at the part where Si and this woman named Julia go to Jake Pickering's office to find out how Jake is connected to Si's girlfriend Kate's grandfather. Si's kind of in love with this 1880s Julia, even though Kate is waiting for him back in the twentieth century. And the other problem is that Julia is engaged to Jake, who's turning out to be a pretty nasty guy. . . ."

Joe's voice trailed off. Lightbulbs were going off in his head. He set his glass down on the table with a loud bang, making both Sam and Wishbone jump.

"I've got it!" Joe announced excitedly. "I know how we can nail whoever's been doing all the damage on the set!"

Hours later, Wishbone tried to settle into a

comfortable position under the bush. "I don't know, Joe. I've worked under better conditions before," he complained, as a sharp branch poked him in the side.

Sam was kneeling next to Wishbone, and Joe was on the other side of Sam. All three of them were hiding in the bushes outside the warehouse that was home to the *Simon Moore* set. It was after eight o'clock, and the sky was getting dark. The air was thick and humid, promising rain.

"Tell me again—*what* are we doing here?" Sam asked Joe. She, too, just like Wishbone, struggled to get into a comfortable position. "It's getting kind of late. . . ."

Wishbone recalled the moment at Pepper Pete's when Joe had come up with his brilliant plan. After lunch, Joe had spent the rest of the afternoon back on the set, appearing in two short scenes—with Wishbone's helpful coaching, of course. Now it was past dinnertime, and everyone had left the warehouse—except for Joe, Sam, and Wishbone.

Joe pulled a snack bar out of his pocket, unwrapped it, and broke it into three pieces. He offered a piece to Sam, and then one to Wishbone.

"Mmm," Wishbone said, munching eagerly.

"It's like I was telling you at lunch," Joe said to Sam. "In *Time and Again,* Si and Julia stake out Jake Pickering's office to find out what's *really* going on between him and Kate's grandfather. That's what we're doing—conducting a stakeout."

Joe popped the piece of snack bar into his mouth.

He told Sam, "It seems as if the culprit does his dirty work at night, when no one else is around. So I thought that if we hung out here long enough, he might show up again."

"Yes, but if I recall, didn't Si and Julia spend the entire night hiding out in Jake's office?" Wishbone reminded Joe. "And they ended up getting trapped in a fire. This stakeout isn't going to end up like that, right, pal? I mean, I'm pretty brave, not to mention fearless, but I draw the line at fires!"

Wishbone sighed and was quiet for a moment. He stared directly at the warehouse.

Then Wishbone said, "Besides, I'd rather be with Phoebe tonight. We had a really romantic evening planned. We were going to take a stroll through Jackson Park, then beg for pizza crusts at Pepper Pete's, then bury toys in Wanda's new rose garden."

Just then, Wishbone's sensitive ears picked up a strange howling noise. It came from far away, but it was still spooky-sounding.

"What was *that?*" he cried out.

"What was *that?*" Sam said.

"Probably just some dog or something," Joe replied, not paying much attention to the noise. "Sam, do you have your camera ready—in case the person shows up?"

Sam patted her backpack, which was at her feet. "It's right here. But Joe, I don't know about this whole idea. It's getting dark, and my dad's going to start worrying about me."

"My feelings exactly," Wishbone said. "Joe, I think you're being outvoted. Let's get *outta* here!"

At that moment, Wishbone's ears picked up another sound. It sounded like footsteps crunching on gravel. And it sounded like the footsteps were coming directly toward them!

Chapter Twelve

Joe ducked down farther in the bushes and put his finger to his lips. *"Shh!* Someone's coming," he whispered to Sam and Wishbone.

Next to him, he could feel Sam trying to scrunch down, too. Out of the corner of his eye, he saw Wishbone flattening himself to the ground like a badger.

The footsteps continued to come closer. Joe tried to see who was there, but it was difficult. Darkness was descending by the minute. Besides that, the bushes were blocking his vision.

Still, despite the darkness, and the bushes that were in the way, Joe could see that the person was a guy. He was tall and slim. Unfortunately, Joe couldn't recognize any details about his face, or anything else about him.

The guy headed for the back door of the warehouse. He unlocked the door, then disappeared inside. As soon as he was out of sight, Joe turned to Sam and whispered, "Did you get a good look at his face?"

"Nope," Sam whispered back. "Did you?"

Joe shook his head. "He didn't look like Fitch, though. Fitch is a lot heavier."

Sam reached into her backpack and pulled out her camera. She checked to make sure there was film inside. Then she made a couple of adjustments for lighting and exposure. "Okay, Mr.-whoever-you-are. I'm ready for you," she said, pointing the camera at the back door of the warehouse.

The three of them waited. The only sounds in the air were strange, distant howls, the soft hum of crickets, and the occasional car driving down the street.

Joe wiped his brow with the back of his hand. It was a hot summer night. Also, as much as he didn't want to admit it, he was nervous about what they were doing. The stakeout was not as tough as the fire that Si Morley had to go through. Still, it was no picnic hiding out in the dark behind a bunch of prickly bushes. . . .

A few minutes later, the guy came back out again. He was carrying what looked to be a cardboard box in his arms. A bunch of large, flat, disk-shaped items were poking out of the top. The disks looked familiar to Joe, but he couldn't tell for sure exactly what they were.

The guy began to walk away from the warehouse, lugging the box.

"He's getting away!" Joe whispered to Sam.

Sam stood up, pointed her camera straight at the guy, and snapped. The flash went off, throwing off a fleeting spark of white light. The guy must have seen it out of his side vision, or maybe he heard the camera go off. He glanced around for a split-second.

In that instant, Sam snapped another picture. "Gotcha!" she muttered under her breath.

The guy turned and began to run, kicking gravel everywhere. He was clearly struggling to balance the heavy box in his arms. A moment later, he disappeared into the darkness.

"Should we try to follow him?" Sam asked Joe, putting the lens cap on her camera.

Joe glanced around, frowning. "I don't think so. It's deserted around here, and he *could* be dangerous."

Joe was holding on to Wishbone's collar. He knew Wishbone would try to chase the man. Wishbone tried to pull away. Like Sam, he seemed to be eager to go after the guy.

"Take it easy, boy. We'll get him another time," Joe told the little dog.

"I guess you're right, Joe," Sam agreed. "I never did get a good look at his face. I'm pretty sure, though, that I got at least one clear shot of it. I'll develop my film first thing tomorrow morning." She popped the roll of film into her backpack. "What were those things he was carrying, anyway?"

"I don't know," Joe replied. "Whatever they were, though, they looked really familiar." He glanced around again and added uneasily, "This place is beginning to give me the creeps. Come on, let's get out of here."

"Come on, Joe. At five-thirty in the morning, the early dog gets the choice pickings at the craft-services table," Wishbone urged, trotting through the warehouse. "'Morning, Bert. 'Morning, Tom," he called out to the crew.

It made Wishbone feel good to know that he was considered a regular on the set now—one of the crew. He was beginning to think that show business was fun—especially with someone like Phoebe around.

"Speaking of which, I wonder where she is. Oh, Phoebe!" She was nowhere to be seen.

Today, Wednesday, they were shooting Simon Moore's first day as mayor of Oakdale. Wishbone's pal, Joe, had a few short lines. An earlier scene—election day, which involved an outside set and lots of extras—was scheduled to be shot later this week, in front of the real Oakdale City Hall.

Joe patted Wishbone on the head and peered around. "I've got to go find Connor and Billy. You stay right here, okay, boy?"

Wishbone looked up at Joe and cocked his head. He knew that his buddy was eager to get to the bottom of last night's incident. Someone had gone into the warehouse after hours and made off with a box of something. The question was who . . . and what . . . and why? It was obviously someone involved with *Simon Moore*, since the person had a key to the warehouse.

"I can't make you any promises," Wishbone said to Joe. "There's a doughnut with my name written on it in the next room. Besides, I have to find Phoebe." His tail wagging, he went on his way.

A few minutes later, after Wishbone had successfully begged for a couple of jelly doughnuts at the craft-services table and finished off one of them, he went to search for Phoebe.

"Oh, Pheebth! I thaved a doughnut for you!" he called out, trying to hold onto a doughnut between his teeth.

As he turned down the hall, he noticed a half-opened dressing-room door. With his super-sensitive ears, he could hear a familiar noise coming from inside: the sound of vigorous chewing.

Wishbone raced over to the door and poked his head inside. He found Phoebe sitting on a pink-silk cushion, gnawing on a delicious-looking toy bone.

Wishbone's heart beat a little faster when he saw Phoebe's face. "Hi," Wishbone said, trotting inside and dropping the doughnut in front of her paws. "Here's a little present for you. Nice place you've got here— Wow! It's *really* nice."

Phoebe's dressing room was small, but nicely furnished. It was just right for a Jack Russell terrier that liked the best of everything. Off in the corner was a comfortable-looking wicker basket that looked like a great place for a nap. Next to it was a big ceramic dish full of kibble, and another one full of water. The floor was covered with dozens of chew toys in assorted shapes, sizes, and colors.

Phoebe dropped her bone, barked joyfully, and got up on all fours. She licked Wishbone's nose and made a contented sound in the back of her throat.

"Aw, Pheebs," Wishbone said, blushing. "It's nice to see you, too."

Phoebe licked his nose again. Then she went over to her sea of toys and selected a beautiful red ball. She pushed it toward Wishbone with her nose. Then she gazed up at him expectantly.

"For *me!*" Wishbone exclaimed. He chased after the ball, grabbed it with his teeth, and bit down into it. It had a terrific rubbery texture, just the way he liked it. "Wow! Phoebe, I'm really touched. You must like me a lot. Which is great, because I like you, too."

The two dogs settled down on the floor side by side. Phoebe gobbled down the jelly doughnut that Wishbone had brought her. Then she went back to chewing on her toy bone. Wishbone did the same with his rubber ball. Every once in a while, Phoebe would glance sideways at him, and Wishbone would feel all warm inside.

"Pheebs," Wishbone said after a while, "what's going to happen when the *Simon Moore* shoot is over? Are you going to go work on another movie somewhere? I bet you are," Wishbone said. "I wish it didn't have to be that way. But I know you really love acting. And you're really good at it, too."

As the two dogs continued to gnaw on their toys, Wishbone's mind was racing. He really didn't want to have to say good-bye to Phoebe when the *Simon Moore* shoot was over. But what was the solution? He couldn't ask her to stay in Oakdale with him, and he couldn't leave Oakdale to go on the road with her.

Or could he?

Joe found Connor and Billy off in a corner of the set, having a tense-looking conversation. A lot of the cast and crew members were standing around, too, talking in hushed voices. None of the actors was in costume or makeup, which was unusual, considering the fact that it was already past six A.M.

I wonder what's going on, Joe thought. *Maybe it has something to do with what happened last night. . . .* Suddenly, he had a really bad feeling in the pit of his stomach.

Joe hurried up to the two brothers. "I need to talk to you both—" he began.

"We need to talk to you, too," Connor interrupted him. He was frowning, and his blue-gray eyes looked troubled. "We're canceling our shoot for today. We're not sure about what's going to happen tomorrow, either."

Joe's jaw dropped. "What? . . . Why?" he managed to say after a moment.

"Our thief has struck again," Billy told him in a grim voice. "Someone came in here last night and stole every last can of film!"

Chapter Thirteen

"What!" Joe gasped. Then it hit him. He now knew what the big, flat disks were that the guy had made off with last night.

He was about to mention to the brothers that he'd witnessed the theft. Then he quickly changed his mind. He wanted to wait until Sam developed her photos. That way, there would be some hard evidence to offer Connor and Billy.

"Anyway, needless to say, we can't shoot without film," Billy went on. He ran a hand through his hair in an irritated way. "I've called our supplier in New York City to send some to us as soon as possible," he went on. "But in the meantime, we've been left high and dry. What a mess!"

"Can't you . . . uh . . . just go to a local store and get some more?" Joe asked weakly.

Connor shook his head. "I'm afraid not, Joe. You can only get this kind of special film in big cities where a lot of movie-making takes place."

Fitch stepped forward, his hands on his hips. He had an angry expression on his face. "This is absolutely outrageous! Are you telling us that we have to put up with yet another scheduling delay because of some prankster you cannot seem to control?"

Some of the other actors and crew members nodded their heads in agreement. Joe noticed that Leo was standing in the background. Unlike the others, Leo seemed to be enjoying the scene unfolding before him.

"I'm not sure anymore that it's just a prankster," Billy said, folding his arms across his chest. "In fact, I think it may be time to bring in the cops—"

"No!" Connor shouted.

Everyone around the set turned to look at him.

"No police," Connor said, more quietly. "We can't afford the bad publicity. *She* would not be happy about it," he added, speaking directly to Billy.

"Oh, yeah. Right." Billy nodded, then fell silent.

She? Are they talking about Mrs. Crabbe? Joe wondered.

Connor turned to talk to Fitch.

Billy wandered over to Joe. He patted Joe on the shoulder and forced a grin. "Hi," he murmured. "Sorry about all this. I'm sure you were expecting a smoother ride on your first big acting job."

"That's okay," Joe said. He felt bad for Billy, and he was disappointed that *Simon Moore* was experiencing so many problems. "Do you have any idea who's responsible for all the stuff that's been happening around here?" he added.

Billy shook his head. "No—that's the problem. I mean, who would be mean enough to do all this stuff

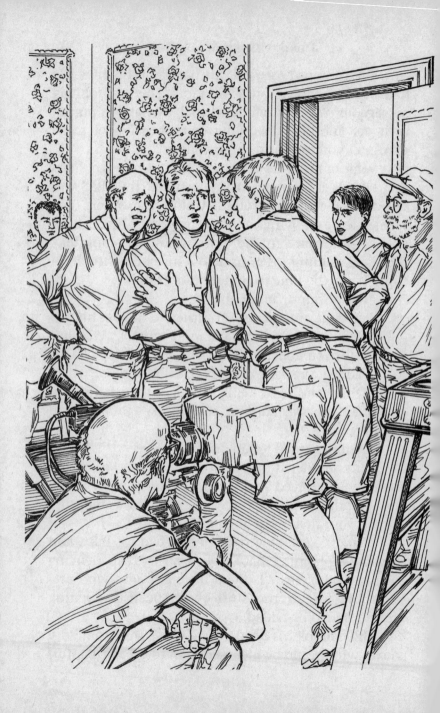

to us? We're just a small, low-budget operation. We're trying to make a good-quality film about a piece of history."

Joe and Billy just looked at each other for a moment, saying nothing.

Billy smiled sadly and added, "This film has been our baby—mine and Connor's—for a really long time. We came up with the idea together in college. Then I wrote the script while we were in film school. Connor spent three years trying to line up funding to make the film. This is our big dream. Now someone's trying to ruin it."

Joe was about to reply when he caught sight of Sam walking toward him. Dressed in shorts, a tank top, and a red baseball cap, she was gesturing wildly for Joe to come over.

"Uh . . . excuse me for a moment," Joe said to Billy.

Then Joe hurried over to where Sam was.

"Hi. What's up?" Joe asked her in a low voice.

In reply, Sam stopped and reached inside her backpack and pulled out a small gray envelope. She dangled it in front of him and grinned.

"Are those the pictures from last night?" Joe asked her eagerly.

"Yes," Sam replied. "I was so psyched, I got up really early this morning to pick them up." She reached into the envelope and pulled out several color photos. "The bad news is, they're a little bit . . . uh . . . fuzzy. The light wasn't great, and the guy was moving."

She handed the pictures to Joe. He studied them.

There were two photos: one of the guy's back, and the other of his body and profile.

Sam was right—the prints *were* fuzzy. Briefly, Joe's mind flashed to *Time and Again*. In addition to having the half-burned letter, Si's girlfriend Kate had another clue in her possession: a strange black-and-white photo, a picture of a nine-pointed star inside of a circle. Si knew that he had to figure out what the photo meant to solve the mystery of Kate's grandfather's suicide. Joe also knew he would have to make sense of Sam's photographs in order to solve *his* mystery.

But the problem was that Sam's photos were unclear, and Joe didn't think he could figure out anything by looking at them.

Joe glanced up at Sam. "This is impossible," he said, discouraged. "There's no way we'll be able to identify the guy from these shots."

Sam smiled. "That's where you're wrong, Joe. I know a specialist who can help us out with this job."

Joe, Sam, and Wishbone stood on the front step of their friend David's house, Even though it was still early in the morning, it was already pretty hot outside. The sky was a bright, cloudless blue, and cicadas hummed shrilly in the trees. A couple of kids from school cycled down the street and waved.

"I hope he's not still sleeping," Sam said, getting ready to ring David's doorbell.

"I thought they were away on vacation," Joe said, puzzled.

"They got back two days ago," Sam replied. "Didn't you get David's messages? He said he tried to call you a couple of times."

"Oh, yeah." Joe recalled vaguely that his mom had given him several messages from David. He'd been so busy thinking about *Simon Moore,* the culprit, and *Time and Again* that he'd completely forgotten to call David back. "So David's the 'specialist' who's going to help us out with these photos, huh?"

Sam wriggled her eyebrows and smiled. "Exactly."

A moment later, David answered the door. He had curly black hair and intelligent brown eyes. He was wearing cutoffs and a baggy purple T-shirt that had the Sequoyah Middle School logo on it.

"Hi, guys. It's great to see you! Come on in," David said cheerfully. "Hey, Joe, can I have your autograph?" he teased. "I hear you're a big movie star now."

"Oh, yeah, right," Joe said, blushing.

"No, really—congratulations!" David said, patting Joe on the back. "I think it's really cool that you're in *Simon Moore.*"

Joe grinned. "Thanks, David."

"So I guess it's all part of being a big movie star, huh? Not returning phone calls?" David was smiling, but he looked a little disappointed, too.

"Oh, yeah—sorry," Joe apologized. "I've been kind of busy."

"I know. Sam filled me in." David gestured for them to go upstairs.

The friends headed up to David's room. Joe always liked to hang out there. David was a whiz when it came

111

to computers, and he had a lot of cool equipment set up in his room.

Joe sat down on the edge of David's bed and pulled Sam's photos out of the envelope. As Wishbone hopped onto the bed, Joe switched on a nearby lamp and held the photos up to the light. He still couldn't make out any telling details.

"So your camping trip was really a lot of fun, David?" Sam said, plopping down next to Joe.

David sat down at his desk and nodded. "It was the best. We cooked all our meals on this super-modern camping stove. And at night, we saw the most awesome constellations." He added, "The place was called Sacandaga Park. Didn't you tell me that you and your dad used to go hiking there, Joe?"

"Hmm . . . ? Oh, yes." Joe leaned across the bed and handed the photos to David. "David, what do you think of these photos? Sam says you can make them clearer."

David took the photos from Joe and studied them in silence. Joe got the impression that David was a little troubled about something. He wondered what was going on with his friend. He would ask him later, after they nailed the person who was trying to ruin *Simon Moore*.

Sam got up from the bed and sat down in a chair next to David. David took one of the photographs—the one of the guy's body and profile—and slid it into a small white plastic box that was next to his computer monitor.

"What's that?" Joe asked David curiously.

"It's a scanner," David replied without turning around. His fingers flew over the keyboard as he punched in a series of commands. "I'm going to scan this photograph into my computer and try to highlight the image," he explained.

After a moment, Sam's photo appeared on the monitor. David punched in several more commands. A bigger version of the photo suddenly appeared on the screen. To Joe, it looked like a wild kaleidoscope of colors.

"Come on, come on," David said, leaning forward in his swivel chair. He continued to type commands, and the photo kept getting longer, wider, sharper. Little dots of color kept rearranging themselves. Joe glanced away for a moment and rubbed his eyes.

"Hey! Check this out!" David said suddenly.

Joe jumped up from the bed and hurried over to the computer. He stared at the screen—and gasped.

David had somehow managed to enlarge and sharpen the photograph to the point where the guy's face was clear enough to be identified.

And if Joe wasn't mistaken, the culprit's face belonged to Billy Drake!

Chapter Fourteen

Joe gaped at David's computer screen. "That's Billy," he said finally. "Billy!" He shook his head. "No way! Why would he be trying to destroy his own movie? I don't understand it!"

Sam explained to David who Billy was. Then she said, "I don't get it, either. But it's definitely him. I mean, look. . . ." Sam pointed to the screen. "He's wearing that baseball cap he always has on."

Joe glanced at the image on the screen again. Even though Sam's photo wasn't one-hundred-percent clear, there was no question that the guy was Billy.

Joe's mind was racing as he considered this bizarre new twist in the ever-growing mystery. Billy would certainly have had the opportunity to do all the stuff that the culprit had been doing: destroying Fitch's costume, writing a threatening note, hiding a bunch of props, calling Wanda Gilmore with an anonymous tip, and stealing all the cans of film.

But what could possibly be Billy's motive? Billy

himself had told Joe that *Simon Moore* was his big dream—his and Connor's. Plus, he was a nice guy.

There's no way he could be the culprit, Joe thought unhappily. And yet, right in front of Joe's eyes was the evidence on David's computer screen, staring him in the face.

"There's got to be a logical explanation here," Joe said out loud. "Maybe someone's forcing Billy to do all this stuff. Maybe it's that woman he and Connor keep talking about—Mrs. Crabbe. And what about Ms. Bradbury?" he added. He recalled the phone number in green ink that he'd found among the stolen props. Just then, Joe had a great idea. He leaned forward and put his hand on David's shoulder. "David, can you get some information for us on the Internet about a couple of people?"

David nodded. "Sure. What people?" Without

missing a beat, he punched in some commands to exit the program he was using and activated his Internet program.

"A woman named Lucy—no, *Lucinda*—Crabbe," Joe replied. "That's it: Lucinda Crabbe. And the other one is Margaret Bradbury."

"Margaret Bradbury!" David exclaimed. "You don't suspect *her*, do you? She's a big wheel with the Windom Foundation. The group gives lots of money to organizations for all kinds of projects."

"I know, I know," Joe said quickly. "But we need to check her out, anyway."

Joe and Sam watched as David typed in a series of commands. "I'm looking for the Windom Foundation's Web site," he murmured. After a few minutes, he glanced up and said, "Look here. The Windom Foundation just gave a ton of money to Oakdale College so it could start a film department."

"*Film* department?" Sam repeated. "Hmm . . . There might be a connection between Ms. Bradbury and *Simon Moore,* after all."

It took David a lot longer to find any information on Lucinda Crabbe. He tried several biographical directories and search-engine programs, but he kept coming up empty.

The three of them were just about to give up when David tapped the screen. "Whoa! Guys! I *really* hit the jackpot!"

Joe's eyes popped open wide. "Really? Why?"

"Don't ask me how, but I finally found her name in this article from the *Indie Daily,*" David said, pointing to the screen. "It's some sort of newspaper about the independent film industry. Anyway, it says here that—get this!—Lucinda Crabbe of New York City is *funding* the making of *Simon Moore*." He turned around and grinned at Joe and Sam. "Your mystery woman, Mrs. Crabbe, is bankrolling this entire production!"

That afternoon, Wishbone ran across the Talbots' front lawn, enjoying the feeling of soft grass beneath his paws. The sun was warming his fur nicely, and the smell of someone's barbecue from last night lingered deliciously in the air.

"Ah, it's good to be alive!" he said happily. "It's good to be a dog! It's good to be me!" He stopped and turned to Joe, who was sitting on a step in front of the house. "Hey, buddy! What do you say we celebrate this special moment with an extra-special game of catch? Maybe we can invite my friend Phoebe to come over and join us."

Joe seemed to be thinking about other things. He had been reading and rereading a passage from a book for the last half-hour. Wishbone knew that it wasn't *Time and Again*. It was a big hardcover that Joe had pulled off one of the living room shelves. It had a dusty, old-book smell that the terrier loved.

Wishbone ran up to Joe and barked a greeting. "Hi, pal! Would you care to share what you're reading with the dog?"

Joe glanced up from his book. "Hi, Wishbone. Solving the mystery that's been happening on the *Simon Moore* set sure is challenging," Joe said.

"Great! The sooner you solve the mystery, the sooner the movie will be finished, and the sooner the wrap party can happen." Wishbone cocked his head. "On the other hand, when the movie's finished, Phoebe will be leaving Oakdale. Oh, problems, problems!"

"I know I should demand an answer from Billy about the stolen film and everything," Joe said slowly, thinking out loud. "But first, I need to figure out what his motive is. Why would he be trying to ruin his own movie?" Then he added, "I have this new hunch. It has to do with the missing last scene of the *Simon Moore* film script."

Joe picked up the crumpled-up piece of the script that he and Wishbone had found along with the stolen props. Clearing his throat, he began to read the dialogue out loud:

"FINNEGAN: Have you reached your decision, yet, Simon?

"SIMON: I've given the matter a great deal of thought. . . .

"BAINBRIDGE: Spare us the details of your soul-searching, *Mayor* Moore. What'll it be?

"SIMON: *(pause)* Gentlemen, I've decided to go ahead with the factory. In fact,"

Wishbone pawed the air eagerly. "Joe, go on and read some more."

"The rest of it is missing," Joe said. He set aside

the piece of paper. "But get this, Wishbone. I was thinking about this business of the factory. The big decision that the *real* Simon Moore had to make was whether to go along with Finnegan and Bainbridge and the rest of those nasty guys and build the factory in the middle of some Oakdale park, right?" His dark eyes gleamed as he added, "Well, there is only one park in Oakdale so they must be talking about Jackson Park, and there is *no* factory there."

Wishbone considered this. "Hmm . . . There's a duck pond, and a T-ball field, and trees and flowers, and a sculpture of the most beloved dog in all of Oakdale: me. But you're right, Joe—there is *no* factory in the middle of Jackson Park."

Joe opened the big hardcover book and jabbed at a page. "And this book confirms it. It says right here: 'In 1882, eighteen-year-old mayor Simon Moore went against his powerful and dishonest town-council members and turned down a proposal for a one-hundred-thousand-square-foot tool factory that was to be built in the middle of what later came to be called Jackson Park. It was a daring and heroic act, and Moore went on to serve three more terms as mayor before leaving political office to become a full-time writer.'"

"A writer! A fine profession!" Wishbone said, wagging his tail.

"It also says here that the tool factory ended up in Wilton," Joe went on. "That's about twenty miles away. It's not even really a town anymore—just factories and warehouses."

"Yes—and no parks for dogs," Wishbone noted.

"Anyway, Billy's script states the opposite," Joe continued. "According to the part of the script I just read, Simon Moore does the exact *opposite* thing—he actually agrees to build the factory in what would become Jackson Park." He added, "So get this: What if Connor or someone else—maybe Margaret Bradbury or Lucinda Crabbe—pressured Billy to change the ending of the movie for some reason? Maybe Billy went along with the demand. But then he decided to destroy the movie rather than see his script changed like that."

"A man of high principles! I like that, although I don't approve of his actions these past few days." Wishbone said.

"It fits with that note, too," Joe said excitedly. "'If the past is changed, this film will never be made.' Billy must have been angry about the fact that Connor or Mrs. Crabbe or whoever was changing the past!"

"Joe, I think you've solved the mystery!" Wishbone jumped up in the air and did a backflip. "Joe? Oh, Joe, where are you going, pal?"

Joe was standing up and stuffing the big history book into his backpack. "Let's get over to the film set right away, Wishbone. I think that it's time to have a talk with Billy!"

Chapter Fifteen

Joe arrived by bike at the *Simon Moore* warehouse a short while later. Wishbone was at his heels. Billy was at the far end of the main room, his cell phone glued to his ear. Joe noticed that Billy wasn't wearing his usual baseball cap.

Billy caught Joe's eye and signaled for him to wait. Connor was nowhere to be seen.

As Joe waited for Billy to get off the phone, he paced restlessly around part of the room. The warehouse was eerily deserted. None of the cast and crew was around. The set for an upcoming scene—Simon Moore's new office—was in place. There was equipment everywhere: lights, cameras, cables, booms.

Joe was amazed by the fact that he had entered this strange new world of film and acting just three days ago. Back then, he had been completely inexperienced. Now, he was as completely at home in the 1880s as Si Morley was in *Time and Again*.

Sam and David, Joe thought. He felt a twinge of

regret at the fact that he hadn't seen much of them lately. Since he'd gotten cast in *Simon Moore,* and all the troubles had started, Joe had been isolated from his two closest friends. *In fact, come to think of it, they've been there for me when I needed them, but I haven't been there for them,* Joe thought. He promised himself to make it up to them—once the mystery was solved and the film shoot was over.

Billy finished his call. Then he walked across the warehouse to where Joe was standing. "Hey, Joe," he called out with a tired-looking smile. "What can I do for you?"

Staring at Billy, Joe was filled with a twinge of regret. Billy had been great to him these last few days, and Joe had really grown to like him. He disliked having to accuse him of a crime—even a crime that he suspected was brought on by well-intentioned principles.

Joe took off his backpack and held it tightly against his chest. He was all too aware of what it contained: the computer-enhanced versions of Sam's photos, showing Billy walking off with the stolen film. . . .

"Joe?" Billy was frowning at him. "Hey, pal, are you okay? You look kind of upset."

Joe shifted uncomfortably from one foot to the other. "Uh . . . I've come to talk to you about something. That is, I've come to talk to you about all the stuff that's been happening on the set."

Billy raised his eyebrows. Then he pointed to a couple of folding chairs. "You wanna take a load off?"

Joe sat down on one of the chairs. Billy sat across from him. Wishbone settled down next to Joe's feet and glanced up at him with anticipation. Joe was glad the little terrier was there; he needed all the moral support he could get.

Joe cleared his throat, then began to speak. Confronting Billy was even more difficult than he'd imagined. "I . . . uh . . . know about the ending of *Simon Moore*," he said slowly. "I know that for some reason, someone made you change the script from the way it really happened."

Billy's eyes looked as though they were going to pop out of his head. "You . . . know?" he said after a moment.

Joe nodded. Then he made himself go on. "When all this stuff started happening on the set, I kind of suspected Fitch was the guilty party," he said. "He had a green ink stain on his hand that matched the green ink on the strange note about changing the past. Plus, I found part of a page from the last scene of your script in the same garbage can that the stolen props were in. It had a phone number written on the back of it—in the same green ink."

Joe stopped for a moment to catch his breath. There was absolute silence in the warehouse. Billy just looked at the floor, not saying a word.

Then Joe went on. "I didn't suspect you until later. See, Sam, Wishbone, and I saw you walk off with the cans of film last night. . . ."

Billy held up his hands. "Whoa! Whoa! Whoa! *Wait* just a second. You're saying *I* stole that film?" he said, with surprise on his face.

"And you destroyed Fitch's costume, and stole the props, and called Miss Gilmore at the *Chronicle* with an anonymous tip about the 'culprit,'" Joe said. "But I understand why you did it," he added quickly. "You were angry about having to change the ending of the film. You were trying to be true to yourself as a writer."

Billy frowned. "Being true to myself as a . . . Joe, what time did you and Sam and Wishbone . . . uh . . . see me take this film?" he asked suddenly.

"About eight o'clock," Joe said, puzzled. "Why?"

"Because I was at Pepper Pete's with Leo and Fitch from about six to nine last night," Billy explained. "You can ask them. We were drowning our production sorrows in a pitcher of soft drinks and a couple of double-pepperoni specials."

Now it was Joe's turn to be stunned. After all this, how could Billy lie to him?

Wishbone nuzzled Joe's leg, encouraging him to go on. Slowly, almost hesitating, Joe pulled the photographs out of his backpack and handed them to Billy. "Sam took these last night. Our friend David

cleaned them up and enlarged them on his computer," Joe explained. He could barely bring himself to look at Billy.

Billy stared at the two photographs. "The baseball cap!" he exclaimed.

"Huh?" Joe said, puzzled.

Billy continued to stare at the photographs. "I don't believe it!" he said finally. "Uh . . . Joe, buddy? This isn't me."

Joe frowned. "What do you mean, it's not you? But if it's not you—"

Then it came to him in a flash. There *was* someone who looked nearly identical to Billy. The baseball cap had thrown Sam and Joe off the track. . . .

"Connor!" Joe and Billy said at the same time. As if on cue, Wishbone began to bark excitedly.

Billy stood up, looking quite upset. "He borrowed my cap yesterday. But I have no idea why he'd do any of this awful stuff to our production." He fished through his pockets, then dangled a set of car keys in the air. "Come on, Joe. We've got to find him—fast!"

After driving to a few spots, Billy, Joe, and Wishbone found Connor at Pepper Pete's. He, Leo, and Fitch were sitting in a booth, sharing a pizza and talking about an upcoming scene. In the background, a sad old song was playing on the jukebox. Most of the late lunch crowd had left, so the place was nearly empty.

"Hi, Joe!" Walter Kepler, Sam's dad, waved from across the restaurant. Joe waved back, but he was distracted. He wasn't looking foward to the scene that was about to take place between Billy and Connor.

"Billy! Joe! Why don't you join us?" Connor said with his typical tight, controlled smile.

Billy marched straight up to his brother. "Connor, *why*?" he demanded.

Connor raised his eyebrows. "Billy, what are you talking about?"

Joe came up behind Billy and set Sam's photos down on the table. He watched Connor's face carefully, waiting for a reaction.

Connor glanced at the photos, then up at Joe and Billy. He was as pale as a ghost. "W-where did these come from?" he said after a long moment.

"My friend Sam took them," Joe replied. "We saw

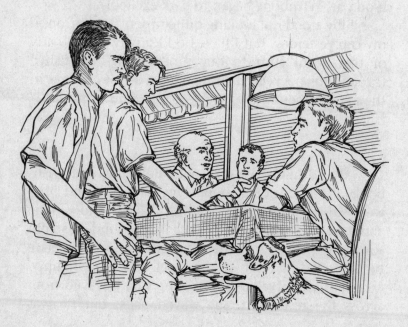

you steal all of those cans of film from the warehouse last night."

"T-that w-was you?" Connor stammered.

"*You* were behind that theft, Connor?" Fitch cried out. He slammed his soft-drink glass on the table with a loud *bang.* "Sir, I demand an explanation!"

"We'd *all* like to hear your story, Connor," Leo said, leaning forward eagerly.

Connor stared at Leo and Fitch and Joe. Then, finally, he worked up the nerve to look at his brother, Billy. Billy looked really angry and hurt. Joe felt sorry for him.

Connor smiled sadly at his brother. Then he turned his glance to the others. "Making *Simon Moore* has been our dream—mine and Billy's—for years," he began. "Billy wrote this amazing script, and we had a number of friends, neighbors, and people we grew up with right here in Oakdale who were willing to work for us for free. The problem was, we still needed a lot of money to finance the production."

"Lucinda Crabbe," Joe said.

Connor raised his eyebrows. "Did Billy tell you— Oh, never mind. Yes, Lucinda Crabbe agreed to finance the film. She lives in New York City, and she loves movies, and she enjoys supporting and encouraging young independent filmmakers." Connor shook his head. "The problem is, she's an extremely demanding and difficult person to deal with. As Billy knows all too well, she won't put up with shooting delays or any kind of negative publicity. And in our case, she also wanted the ending of the film changed."

"But why? The real ending is powerful," Leo

127

spoke up. "You know, Simon Moore has the courage to stand up to the bad guys for the good of his town. He is a hero!"

Connor nodded. "You'll get no argument from me there. But Lucinda Crabbe thought it was too 'Hollywood,' or something like that. She wanted the film to be a tragedy—to show the downfall of a great American hero."

Wishbone circled several times and lay down at Joe's feet. Joe leaned down and scratched his ears. Wishbone's tail began to thump.

"Billy agreed to write a new ending, even though it upset him greatly to see his story changed around like that," Connor went on. He turned to Billy. "I know you were doing it as a favor to me, because you knew how much I wanted to see *Simon Moore* get made and shown to audiences." He smiled and shrugged. "Well, Billy, I decided to repay the favor. I came up with a plan to try to line up another source of funding for the movie without letting you know."

Billy gasped. *"What?"*

"Margaret Bradbury," Joe said, finally understanding. When Connor stared at him in surprise, Joe told him about the phone number he'd found on the script page that was with the missing props.

"Ms. Bradbury is considering having the Windom Foundation finance the entire production of the film," Connor explained to Billy and the others. "That was the important meeting I had yesterday. I've been getting together with her for a while now, trying to negotiate a firm deal.

"But in the meantime, I had to try to delay the

shoot as much as I could, without having anyone suspect what I was up to. There was still the possibility that the foundation wouldn't come through with the money. Then we'd have to fall back on Lucinda Crabbe's funding. That's why I insisted that we keep the last scene a secret. I felt I had to do everything I could to slow down the shooting schedule. . . ."

"Including destroying Fitch's costume, hiding the props, writing a threatening note, and stealing the cans of film," Joe said. He added, "I heard you and Billy talking about some phone call you got from some guy. What was that all about?"

"There *was* no phone call. I told Billy that days ago, just to spook him into thinking that someone was threatening to interfere with the production. I wanted to set the stage for the 'culprit.'" Connor turned to Billy with a heavy sigh. "I know this wasn't the best way to get *Simon Moore* made, Billy. I just didn't know what else to do. I suppose you're furious at me."

"Furious? No." Billy sat down next to his brother and stared at him for a long moment. Then he clasped him in a warm hug. "You're crazy," he said, his voice cracking with emotion. "I can't believe you did all this just to give me back my original ending. You should have just talked to me. We would have figured something out."

"Well . . . maybe . . . but I'm not so sure." Connor smiled apologetically at his brother. "So you forgive me, Billy?"

"It's not *my* forgiveness you have to worry about," Billy replied. "You'd better start with Leo and Fitch and Joe, here. After that, you still have a lot of explaining to do to a lot of other people who've been counting on us in this project. . . ."

As Joe watched the two brothers, he thought about their relationship. Connor struck everyone as sour and interested only in himself, while Billy was seen as the kind, good-natured one. It would have made more sense for Billy to have made some grand gesture for Connor's benefit . . . not the other way around.

I guess people can be full of surprises, Joe thought.

Then Joe remembered a couple of unsolved issues. "Connor?" he said out loud. "What about the note and the phone number in green ink? Fitch had the same color ink on his hand the other day."

"I'm afraid I . . . uh . . . took his pen," Connor explained, somewhat embarrassed.

"I *wondered* where that thing had disappeared to," Fitch said.

"And another thing," Joe went on. "What about the anonymous phone call to Miss Gilmore?"

Connor frowned. "You mean the woman at the *Chronicle?* She told me about the anonymous call, but I was not the one responsible for it."

"Then who . . ." Billy murmured.

Leo turned to gaze out the window, whistling softly. He suddenly seemed very busy watching the traffic go by on Main Street.

Joe stared at Leo. It was all coming back to him now—his conversation with the actor several days ago about the positive benefits of negative publicity.

"Leo!" Joe cried out. "*You* were the one who called Miss Gilmore. I should have figured that out sooner!"

Wishbone got up on all fours and let out a loud bark, as if to back up Joe's statement.

Leo whirled around. "What? Me?" he said innocently. When he saw that Fitch, Connor, Billy, and Joe were all glaring at him, a blush crept across his cheeks. "Oh, all right," he mumbled. "So I did it. I was just trying to boost my . . . I mean, boost the *film* . . . by stirring up some publicity."

"Oh, boy, what a mess," Billy said, shaking his head.

"It's a good thing Miss Gilmore is too honest a journalist to have fallen for your tricks," Connor said. Then his expression softened, and he broke into a grin. "But, then again, who am I to judge you for playing tricks? Obviously, we all need to start fresh. A brand-new beginning for *Simon Moore,* with no tricks or secret endings or deceptions. . . ."

"Agreed," Billy said happily. He lifted a glass of soft drink and raised it in the air. "And may the Windom Foundation come through with our money so we can be true to the history of the *real* Simon Moore!"

Wishbone barked and did a backflip. Joe laughed and patted his pal on the head. For the first time in days, he felt that everything might turn out all right, after all.

Chapter Sixteen

"Scene Twenty-four, Take Six."

"Everyone settle—and action!"

Two days later, Joe, Sam, David, and Wishbone watched from across the street as Connor set the scene in motion. A horse-drawn carriage crossed in front of city hall and stopped. At the same time, Leo Karras came out from inside the building with a pretty, young woman—Simon Moore's wife—on his arm. A crowd of extras—people hired for a small fee to appear in a group scene—who were standing on the sidewalk cheered, and Leo waved. Connor was shooting the last and final scene.

As Joe watched the scene progress, he thought about the events of the last few days. The day after he and Billy had confronted Connor, Connor had confessed everything to the *Simon Moore* cast and crew. He apologized to everyone for his actions.

Leo had done the same thing. He also cleared everything up with Wanda Gilmore.

At the same time, news came from Ms. Bradbury that the Windom Foundation would be willing to finance the entire production—with Billy's original ending remaining in the script.

Joe, too, had done some apologizing—to his best friends Sam and David. He realized that he had been so caught up in *Simon Moore* and the mystery of what was happening on the set that he hadn't been much of a friend to them. He'd not been supportive of Sam when she'd tried to get his input on her portfolio. And he'd neglected to return David's calls, or show the least bit of interest in his camping trip.

Sam and David had come through for him, even though he'd not been a good friend. They had both helped him solve the mystery of the culprit on the movie set.

And now everything's back to normal, Joe thought happily. *Better than normal—great!*

Joe felt very fortunate and happy that he'd been a part of the making of *Simon Moore*. But now that the shoot was almost over, he felt kind of relieved. He'd learned a lot, and he'd met some interesting people, too. But he was really much more at home on the basketball court . . . or even in Mr. Gurney's used-book store, where he had a terrific summer job surrounded by thousands of great old books.

A moment later, Leo got into the carriage with the actress playing his wife and drove away. Connor took off his baseball cap—it was his now, for Billy had given it to him for permanent good luck—and tossed it in the air. "Cut! That's a wrap! Gang, we're *done!*" he shouted with glee.

The crowd of cast, crew, and extras cheered wildly. Connor and Billy shared a victorious hug.

Phoebe came trotting up to Wishbone. The two of them began to bark, adding to the festive, chaotic mood.

Sam and David turned to Joe, and the three friends exchanged high-fives.

"Now, what?" Sam cried out.

"Now it's time to get ready for the wrap party!" Joe said with a grin.

Wishbone put his paws up on the table at Pepper Pete's. "Let's see . . . . Pepperoni, sausage, or all veggie?" he considered. "I don't know, Pheebs. What do you think?"

Wishbone and Phoebe were at the evening wrap party for *Simon Moore.* Pepper Pete's was filled with the cast and crew, plus some friends and family members, too. Joe was sitting at one of the big tables with his mom, Miss Gilmore, David, and Sam. A loud rock song from the 1980s—not the 1880s—was playing on the jukebox.

Phoebe put her paws next to Wishbone's and sniffed at the pizza offerings. Wishbone wagged his tail. "I think what you're trying to tell me, Pheebs, is that you think we should try one of each flavor," he said. "No problem. I'll arrange for it."

Walter Kepler noticed Wishbone and Phoebe at the banquet table and slipped them a couple of pizza slices on a paper plate. "Here you go," he said, setting the plate on the floor.

"Thanks, Walter," Wishbone said. "We won't forget you at the end of the evening."

After he and Phoebe had gobbled down the slices, Wishbone sat down and faced her. He felt a lump in his throat, and it wasn't from eating the pizza too fast.

"I know we've been putting off this little talk," Wishbone said to Phoebe after a moment. "The shoot is over, and you'll be going away soon."

Phoebe cocked her head and looked at him.

"I know, I'm sad, too," Wishbone told her. "For a while, I thought that maybe you might want to stick around in Oakdale and live with me and Joe and Ellen. Oakdale's a really great town for dogs—there's Pepper Pete's, and Jackson Park, and Pepper Pete's, and Wanda's garden, and Pepper Pete's. . . ."

Wishbone paused, got up on all fours, and moved closer to the other terrier.

"But I know I can't ask you to give up your acting life," he went on. "I used to think show business was pretty awful, especially after my experience as Mr.

MacPooch. But now, I realize that it doesn't have to be like that. And I know you really love acting."

Phoebe gazed at him. Looking back into her big, mud-puddle-colored eyes, Wishbone felt a momentary pang of weakness. But he knew he had to be honest with her. It was the only way.

"I also thought about giving up my life in Oakdale and going on the road with you," he said finally. "But I know now that it's not possible. I belong here with Joe and Ellen and the gang—just the way you belong in your world." Wishbone took a close look at Phoebe and wagged his tail. "Come on, let's go over to Joe's table and beg for some more pizza. We have a few hours left together—let's make the most of them!"

Phoebe gave a joyful little bark. She gave Wishbone a gentle lick on his nose. Then the two dogs trotted over to Joe's table.

"Hi, gang," Wishbone greeted everyone. "Got any leftovers for the two hungry dogs? By the way, has everyone met my best friend, Phoebe? My *canine* best friend, that is," he added, for Joe's benefit.

Joe was busy telling his mom and Miss Gilmore and his friends about *Time and Again.* "I finally finished it last night," he was saying. "It was a good story, but you will have to read it yourselves if you want to know the ending."

Ellen put her hand on Joe's arm. "I'm really glad you enjoyed *Time and Again,* Joe. It was one of many of your dad's favorite mysteries."

"And now it's one of mine," Joe said with a smile.

Just then, Billy and Connor came up to the table. "Howdy, everyone," Billy called out. Then he turned to

Joe. "Listen, I just wanted to thank you again for being in *Simon Moore*. And, more important, I want to thank you for making my crazy brother come to his senses."

Laughing, Billy threw his arm around Connor's shoulder and pretended to squeeze it really hard.

Connor laughed, too. Wishbone's ears perked up in disbelief. It was the first time he'd ever heard the director laugh!

"Same goes for me, Joe," Connor added. "I really appreciate everything you did for us."

"No problem," Joe said. "Being in this movie has been a lot of fun. Just make sure to invite us all to the premiere, okay?"

"It'll be the party of the century," Billy promised.

The brothers waved good-bye. Then they headed over to a booth where Leo, Fitch, and some of the other actors were sitting.

"It looks as if we're out of pizza," Joe noted. "What do you say I go over to the buffet table and get us some more?" He stood up and started to walk across the room.

"History, mystery, and seconds on pizza—what more could a dog want?" Wishbone said, his tail thumping. "Joe, let me give you a paw with that! Come on, you, too, Pheebs!"

The two dogs went trotting happily after Joe.

About Nancy Butcher

Nancy Butcher is the author of fourteen children's books, including four Ghostwriter mysteries (*Daycamp Nightmare, Disaster on Wheels, Creepy Sleepaway,* and *Caught in the Net*). *Lights! Camera! Action Dog!* is her second WISHBONE book; her first was *Dr. Jekyll and Mr. Dog,* which she wrote for The Adventures of Wishbone series. She has also written a number of short stories for the Bepuzzled/Spider Tales series, a radio play for kids, and some essays and short stories for adults.

Nancy discovered *Time and Again* on her bookshelf one day. She sat down and began to read it, then couldn't stop until she finished the story. She loved its blend of history, mystery, time-travel, and romance, not to mention all the twists and turns and plot surprises. Author Jack Finney's wonderful storytelling ability made Nancy feel as if she had been transported to another place and time. It's the same feeling she gets every time she watches a WISHBONE episode or reads a WISHBONE book.

Nancy lives in Saratoga Springs, New York, with her husband, Philip Reynolds; their three-year-old son, Christopher; and their three cats, Fanny, Ming, and Mouse. Nancy loves Saratoga Springs because it has a rich historical past, fine Victorian architecture, and a small-town atmosphere.

Like Simon Moore, the fictional mayor of 1880s Oakdale, Nancy is involved in a protest against a new real estate development—a shopping complex the size of four football fields—that threatens to ruin the special character of her town.

Nancy and her family would love to add a cute little dog like Wishbone to their household. But the cats have voted no, so the dog decision is on hold—at least for now.

Now Playing on Your VCR...

Two exciting **Wishbone®** stories on video!

Ready for an adventure? Then leap right in with **Wishbone™** as he takes you on a thrilling journey through two great action-packed stories. First, there are haunted houses, buried treasure, and mysterious graves in two back-to-back episodes of *A Tail in Twain*, starring **Wishbone** as Tom Sawyer. Then, no one is more powerful than Hercules...or rather **Wishbone**, in *Hercules Unleashed*, featuring exciting new footage! It's more fun than a flea dip! It's **Wishbone** on home video.

Available wherever videos are sold.

The Adventures of WISHBONE™

Read all the books in
The Adventures of Wishbone™ series!

Read all the books in the
WISHBONE™ Mysteries series!

WHAT HAS FOUR LEGS, A HEALTHY COAT, AND A GREAT DEAL ON MEMBERSHIP?

IT'S THE **WISHBONE ZONE**™
THE OFFICIAL **WISHBONE**™ FAN CLUB!

When you enter the **WISHBONE ZONE,** you get:
- Color poster of **Wishbone**™
- **Wishbone** newsletter filled with photos, news, and games
- Autographed photo of **Wishbone** and his friends
- **Wishbone** sunglasses, and more!

To join the fan club, pay $10 and charge your **WISHBONE ZONE** membership to VISA, MasterCard, or Discover. Call:

1-800-888-WISH

Or send us your name, address, phone number, birth date, and a check for $10 payable to Big Feats! (TX residents add $.83 sales tax/IN residents add $.50 sales tax). Write to:

WISHBONE ZONE
P.O. Box 9523
Allen, TX 75013-9523

Prices and offer are subject to change. Place your order now!